He knows. He'[...]
blank if Emily i[...]
be able to lie...

"Tess?"

She turned toward Jared, her hand at her heart. In spite of her trepidation, a secret thrill raced through Tess. She couldn't deny that she still felt something for Jared Spencer. But there was danger in the temptation he offered her. If she let Jared back into her life, the serpent would be sure to follow.

He gave her a bemused look. "Why are you staring at me like that?"

She pushed a lock of hair behind her ear and relaxed. He didn't know about Emily. He couldn't. "I'm just surprised to see you, that's all."

He smiled at her, and Tess's heart began to pound in earnest. She was a grown woman, for goodness' sake. She shouldn't be reacting so strongly to a good-looking man.

But of course, Jared wasn't just any man. He was her daughter's father. That alone made him irresistibly sexy.

Dear Harlequin Intrigue Reader,

Welcome again to another action-packed month of exceptional romantic suspense. We are especially pleased to bring you the first of a trilogy of new books from Rebecca York's 43 LIGHT STREET series. You've loved this author and her stories for years...and—you ain't seen nothin' yet! The MINE TO KEEP stories kick off this month with *The Man from Texas*. Danger lurks around every corner for these heroes and heroines, but there's no threat too great when you have the one you love by your side.

The EDEN'S CHILDREN miniseries by Amanda Stevens continues with *The Tempted*. A frantic mother will fight the devil himself to find her little girl, but she'll have to face a more formidable foe first—the child's *secret* father.

Adrianne Lee contributes a terrific twin tale to the DOUBLE EXPOSURE promotion. Look for *His Only Desire* and see what happens when a stalker sees double!

Finally, Harper Allen takes you on a journey of the heart in her powerful two-book miniseries, THE AVENGERS. *Guarding Jane Doe* is a profound story about a soldier for hire and a woman in desperate need of his services. What they find together is everlasting love the likes of which is rarely—if ever—seen.

So join us once again for a fantastic reading experience.

Enjoy!

Sincerely,

Denise O'Sullivan
Associate Senior Editor
Harlequin Intrigue

THE TEMPTED
AMANDA STEVENS

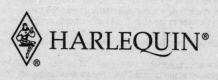

HARLEQUIN®

TORONTO • NEW YORK • LONDON
AMSTERDAM • PARIS • SYDNEY • HAMBURG
STOCKHOLM • ATHENS • TOKYO • MILAN • MADRID
PRAGUE • WARSAW • BUDAPEST • AUCKLAND

ISBN 0-373-22626-8

THE TEMPTED

Copyright © 2001 by Marilyn Medlock Amann

Visit us at www.eHarlequin.com

Printed in U.S.A.

ABOUT THE AUTHOR

Born and raised in a small, Southern town, Amanda Stevens frequently draws on memories of her birth-place to create atmospheric settings and casts of eccentric characters. She is the author of over twenty-five novels, the recipient of a Career Achievement Award for Romantic/Mystery, and a 1999 RITA finalist in the Gothic/Romantic Suspense category. She now resides in Texas with her husband, teenage twins and her cat, Jesse, who also makes frequent appearances in her books.

Books by Amanda Stevens

HARLEQUIN INTRIGUE
373—STRANGER IN PARADISE
388—A BABY'S CRY
397—A MAN OF SECRETS
430—THE SECOND MRS. MALONE
453—THE HERO'S SON*
458—THE BROTHER'S WIFE*
462—THE LONG-LOST HEIR*
489—SOMEBODY'S BABY
511—LOVER, STRANGER
549—THE LITTLEST WITNESS**
553—SECRET ADMIRER**
557—FORBIDDEN LOVER**
581—THE BODYGUARD'S ASSIGNMENT
607—NIGHTTIME GUARDIAN
622—THE INNOCENT†
626—THE TEMPTED†

*The Kingsley Baby
**Gallagher Justice
†Eden's Children

Don't miss any of our special offers. Write to us at the following address for information on our newest releases.

Harlequin Reader Service
U.S.: 3010 Walden Ave., P.O. Box 1325, Buffalo, NY 14269
Canadian: P.O. Box 609, Fort Erie, Ont. L2A 5X3

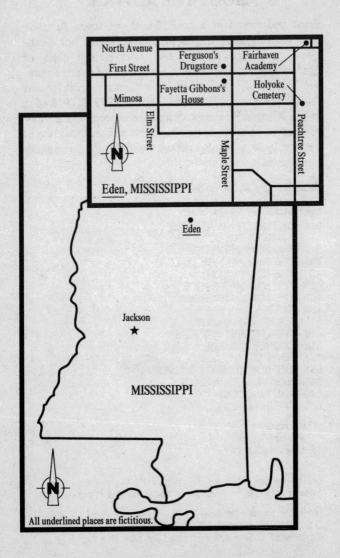

North Avenue

First Street

Mimosa

Ferguson's
Drugstore •

Fayetta Gibbons's
House

Fairhaven
Academy

Holyoke
Cemetery •

Elm Street

Maple Street

Peachtree Street

Eden, MISSISSIPPI

• Eden

Jackson ★

MISSISSIPPI

All underlined places are fictitious.

CAST OF CHARACTERS

Tess Campbell—Her little girl is missing, and in order to find her, Tess may have to reveal a secret she swore she'd take to her grave.

Jared Spencer—Six years ago, Tess left town without a backward glance. Now she's walked back into his life, but before he succumbs to temptation, Jared has to know the truth about that night.

Royce Spencer—Taught all his life that winning is the only thing that matters, he will do anything to best his older brother, Jared.

Ariel Spencer—Is she frightened of her husband, or is she a willing accomplice in his dangerous machinations?

Cressida Spencer—She knows the sort of woman she wants for her son, and Tess Campbell is *not* the one.

Melanie Kent—One of the few people who knows Tess's secret, she paid a huge price six years ago for her involvement with Royce Spencer.

Willa Banks—A dedicated volunteer or a suspect?

This book is gratefully dedicated to my editor,
Denise O'Sullivan, without whom EDEN'S CHILDREN
would not have been possible.

Prologue

"Mama?" Five-year-old Emily Campbell sat up in bed and rubbed her eyes as she tried to peer through the darkness. Someone was sitting beside her bed.

"Your mother's not here. Go back to sleep."

"I want my mama."

"She's not here, I said. Now hush."

Emily began to cry. "I want to go home. Why can't I go home?"

"Because your mother had to go away for a while, so she asked me to look after you. Remember? I told you that."

Yes, but Emily still didn't believe it. Her mama would never go away and leave her for this long. Where was she? Where was Grandma JoJo? Why hadn't they come for her? A terrifying thought struck Emily. What if something had happened to them?

"I'm scared," she whimpered.

"Why are you scared? You're not hurt, are you? You're not sick. I'm taking real good care of you, just like I promised I would. And look at all these pretty dolls...I got them just for you."

It was true. Emily hadn't been hurt. She'd been taken care of, although sometimes she was left alone for long periods of time, locked in this room. And she did have lots of toys to play with. They just weren't her toys.

"Can I have Brown Bear?" she asked in a tiny voice.

A soft, cuddly toy was placed in her arms, but Emily pushed it away. "I want *my* Brown Bear."

A frustrated sigh. "Are we going to have to go through this every night?"

Emily began to wail. "I want my Brown Bear! I want my mama!"

"Stop that!"

A hand touched Emily's shoulder in the darkness, and she tried to flinch away.

"I'm not going to hurt you. It's a picture of your mother. Put it under your pillow and it'll make you feel all better."

The picture was slipped into her hand, but Emily didn't want it. She didn't want it anywhere near her. The lady in that photograph wasn't her mother, no matter how many times she was told differently.

"Look at your mama. Isn't she pretty?"

"That's not my mama."

"Sure it is. It's just been so long since you saw her, you've forgotten what she looks like, that's all."

It *had* been a long time since Emily had seen her mother. So very long. But she still remembered what her mother looked like. She had long, glorious hair, just like the lady in the fairy tale Emily loved so much, and a smile that made Emily feel all warm inside. The woman in the picture looked nothing like Emily's mother.

But she didn't put up a fuss this time. She took the picture and stuffed it underneath her pillow without a word because she didn't want the light to be turned on.

In the dark, she could make believe this really was her room, and that her mother was just down the hallway.

Sniffing back her tears, Emily lay down and curled up beneath the covers, closing her eyes and pretending to fall back asleep. She tried to imagine her mama sitting beside her on the bed, reading to her from the book that had been Emily's favorite since she was little. "Good night, Mama," she whispered, so softly no one in the darkness could hear her.

Chapter One

Eden, Mississippi

Tess Campbell sat in the Jefferson County Sheriff's Office and tried very hard not to scream. Her nails dug into her palms as she listened in despair to the explanation of why the search for her five-year-old daughter, who had been missing for almost three weeks, was being scaled back.

The small office was crowded with law enforcement personnel and others involved in the search, but the only one who seemed capable of making eye contact with Tess at the moment was Naomi Cross, who worked for the Children's Rescue Network, an organization founded to help parents of missing and exploited children.

Of all the people in the room, Naomi was the only one who truly understood Tess's agony because Naomi's own daughter had vanished ten years ago, the victim of an abduction with bizarre similarities to Emily's.

Naomi had been a lifeline to Tess during the days following Emily's disappearance. She'd provided the kind of emotional support and common-sense advice that only someone who had been through the same kind of hell could offer. But there was nothing Naomi could say or do now to ease Tess's torment. Her only child was still missing, and the police were giving up. They'd written her off. Emily would now become another statistic.

Tess's stomach knotted with tension. Each step of the investigation had brought its own special agony—the terror and panic during the initial, frenzied canvassing of the area around the school when her daughter had first gone missing, the pity Tess had seen in the eyes of the other parents as they'd try to reassure her that Emily would be found, safe and sound.

The second day had brought another parade of horrors as the ground search had been widened into the countryside. Bloodhounds had been brought in and divers had gone into the lake while Tess had waited helplessly by the phone.

But, then, the next step had brought renewed hope. Volunteers from all over the state began pouring in to help in the search, and a command center was set up to process incoming and outgoing information. The National Crime Information Center was alerted so that every law enforcement body in the country would have an accurate description of Emily in the event that someone might spot her.

Then came more waiting. More praying.

The national registries for missing and exploited children were notified.

And as the search progressed, a new reality had slowly settled over Tess. The terror and panic of those first few hours, the disbelief and lingering hope of the next several days eventually metastasized into a deep, seeping dread. Emily might not be coming back. Ever.

Tess had once heard someone on TV, another grieving mother, describe the disappearance of her child as a slow, torturous death. But it was worse than death to Tess because there was no finality, no acceptance. No goodbye. Just a nagging hole inside her heart that grew larger and larger with each passing day.

And now the next step had arrived. The search and investigation were being cut back.

"Don't misunderstand me, Tess," Sheriff Mooney was saying. "There's not a man or woman in this department who won't remain dedicated to finding Emily. But we have to be realistic. The volunteers have families and jobs they have to get back to, and we have other cases. We just don't have the manpower or the resources to continue an all-out search."

Tess closed her eyes, mustering her courage, clinging with every ounce of her strength to the belief that her daughter was still alive. "You can't give up," she said hoarsely. "She's still alive! I know she is. I can feel it." Her gaze shot to the photographs of Sheriff Mooney's grandchildren mounted on the wall behind his desk. "What if it was one of them? Would you give up then?"

The sheriff flinched, as if her words cut a little too close to the quick. "We're not giving up, Tess. That's not what I'm saying."

"It sure sounds like it to me," she said bitterly. "What about the FBI?"

"They'll continue to advise and offer technical support on the case, just as they have been. That won't change."

"But they won't be a presence in the investigation, will they? They won't leave an agent in Eden, because they're giving up, too." Tess leaned forward, her fists clenched so tightly her nails cut into her skin. But she welcomed the pain. It kept her focused. It kept her angry, and that was exactly what she needed at the moment.

She couldn't afford to give in to her grief, to the bone-chilling terror that had racked her since Emily disappeared from that playground ten years to the day Naomi Cross's child had gone missing from the same schoolyard.

No trace of Sadie Cross had ever been found, and the date of the abductions, along with the physical resemblance of the two girls and the similarities in their backgrounds, had prompted the police to theorize that the same kidnapper had taken both children.

But then two days after Tess's daughter disappeared, Sara Beth Brodie, one of Emily's kindergarten classmates, had been abducted from a nearby drugstore. She'd been found safe and sound a few days later, and as it turned out, her kidnapping was unrelated to the other two. But her rescue had buoyed Tess's hopes just the same. Didn't the police understand that Sara Beth's safe return meant that Emily could still be found, too?

Or were they more convinced than ever that Emily had met the same fate as Sadie Cross? That ten years from now, no trace of Tess's daughter would have turned up, either?

But there was a difference in the two cases. A week after Emily's disappearance, a note had been discovered on the windshield of a vehicle parked in Tess's driveway. The message, apparently written by a child, read: *I come home soon mama.*

Those words tore at Tess's heart, gave her yet another faint ray of hope to cling to. Emily was still alive.

She was still out there somewhere. The police couldn't stop looking for her now. They *couldn't*.

"What about the note?" She forced herself to speak in a rational tone, even though her mind raged against the terrible images of her daughter, alone and hurt, crying out for her mother. "It has to mean something."

Lieutenant Dave Conyers, the lead detective on Emily's case had been standing across the room staring out the window ever since Tess arrived. He was a tall man, thin, good-looking, with dark hair and piercing blue eyes. He turned now and faced her.

Like everyone else present, he looked exhausted, haggard and guilt-ridden, his face revealing all too plainly that he wished he were anywhere in the world but here in the same room with Tess. "I told you what the results were from the crime lab. They ran all kinds of tests on the paper, including electrostatic detection. A partial fingerprint was detected under ultraviolet, but when we scanned the print and ran it through the database, we didn't get a hit. Nor was it Emily's."

Emily had been fingerprinted and issued a photo ID containing all her vital statistics her first year in preschool. The program had been conducted by Naomi Cross's group, the Children's Rescue Network, to aid the police in just such a contingency. Tess had readily agreed to participate in the effort, but she'd never thought she would actually need the card. No parent did.

"We also had a handwriting expert compare the note with some of Emily's school papers," Lieutenant Conyers continued. "But his analysis was inconclusive. I hate like hell to say this, but the note could be a hoax."

"No!" Tess said stubbornly. "I don't believe that. It was from Emily. I know it was."

"That's what you want to believe. That's what we all want to believe, but the expert couldn't make that determination. Evidently, printing, especially by a child as young as Emily, is a lot harder to analyze than cursive writing." He glanced at Tess. "You're Emily's mother, and you weren't so certain at first the note was from her."

"I know, but maybe that's because she had to write it under duress. She was scared. Even an adult's handwriting would be affected under similar circumstances."

"That's true enough," Conyers agreed. "But the note itself doesn't make much sense when you think about it. A message from a kidnapper is usually either a ransom demand or a taunt to the police or to the child's parents. Why would the kidnapper allow Emily to write such a note, and then risk being caught by delivering it?"

"I don't know," Tess said numbly. "To let me know that she's alive?"

No one said anything, but Tess could sense their doubt. And on some level, she knew Lieutenant Conyers was right. The note didn't make sense. For one thing, it had been placed on the windshield of Naomi Cross's Jeep Cherokee instead of Tess's Ford Explorer. Naomi had been to see Tess that day, and her vehicle had been the only one in the driveway because Tess's was parked in the garage. The SUVs were so similar in color that the initial assumption was that the kidnapper had mistaken Naomi's vehicle for Tess's, even though Tess's was a much older model.

But maybe that wasn't the case. Maybe someone had deliberately put the note on Naomi's car to torment her as well as Tess.

Could anyone really be that cruel or that sick?

A day ago, Tess wouldn't have believed it possible to plunge any deeper into despair. But now that the search for Emily was being scaled down, now that everyone else was going back to their normal lives, she knew what it felt like to be truly alone and helpless. This, the final step, was perhaps the most agonizing of all.

Something of her anguish must have shown on her face because Sergeant Abby Cross, a detective in the Criminal Investigations Unit and Naomi's sister, said gently, "I know how all this must sound to you, Tess, but in spite of the setbacks, the search will continue. Calls are still trickling in on the hotline, and we'll follow them up. We won't give up on Emily. We won't forget about her."

Abby shoved back a lock of dark, glossy hair as she stared at Tess. She wasn't as beautiful as her sister, Naomi, nor as tall and willowy, but there was compassion in her brown eyes. A softness in her smile in spite of her years in law enforcement.

Tess had liked Abby at once, and she wanted to believe her now. Wanted to take solace in Abby's assurances. She was a good cop. With the help of an ex-FBI profiler, she'd cracked the Sara Beth Brodie case. She was working on Emily's case now, and Tess wished that she was in charge instead of Dave Conyers. Abby had found Sara Beth. Maybe she could find Emily, too.

But in ten years, not even Abby Cross had been able to locate Sadie, her own niece, and Naomi had been forced to endure that slow death, to exist in the terrible purgatory of never knowing what had happened to her child.

One by one, Tess studied the faces around her, and she knew that the same thought was paramount on everyone's mind. In the last ten years, three of Eden's children had gone missing. Only one of them had returned. If they didn't find Emily, if they never determined what had happened to Sadie, how many more children would be taken? How many more parents would have to suffer?

"TESS, WAIT A MINUTE!"

Tess had been heading across the parking lot to her car, but she paused now as someone called out her name. Turning, she saw Naomi Cross hurry across the asphalt toward her. Even from a distance, even in her despair, Tess marveled at the woman's extraordinary beauty. She was tall and thin, with a flawless complexion and large brown eyes rimmed with thick lashes. She looked like a model as she hurried across the parking lot toward Tess.

By comparison, Tess knew her own looks had suffered since her daughter's disappearance, so much so she hardly recognized herself in the mirror these days. She'd lost weight, and her face, thin to begin with, now appeared pale and gaunt. Her blue eyes were shadowed with grief and exhaustion, and her hair hung in a limp ponytail down her back. For Tess, makeup and hair appointments had become a thing of the past. It was all she could do to drag herself out of bed each morning and get dressed.

But it was more than Naomi Cross's looks that provided a stark contrast. She exuded a strength and quiet dignity, garnered from her tragedy, that Tess knew she would never be able to muster.

Naomi stopped beside Tess and placed a hand on her arm. "Are you okay?"

Tess let out a ragged breath. "No. How could I be, after what they just told me in there?"

"I know what you're feeling," Naomi said gently. "When it first happens, you think nothing could be worse than learning your child has disappeared. But then comes the day when the police stop actively searching for her. When the volunteers all go home, the command center is shut down, and your daughter becomes just another face on a milk carton. Life returns to normal for everyone but you." Naomi paused. "That's when your faith is most sorely tested."

Tess wrapped her arms around her middle. "I'm not sure I have any faith left." She searched the early-morning sky. White clouds scattered across an intense, blinding blue, and the sun hovered in the east. It was late August, still hot and humid, the temperature marching steadily upward to the nineties. But in spite of the heat, Tess thought she could detect a hint of fall in the air. Or maybe it was her mood. Maybe it was a portent. The seasons would be changing soon. Would her daughter still be missing?

"I want her to come home. I want to hold her in my arms again. She's just a baby. She didn't deserve this. How could something like this happen?" she asked angrily.

When Naomi reached a hand to touch her arm, Tess flinched away. Immediately remorse set in. Naomi had been nothing but kindness. "I'm sorry," Tess whispered, putting a trembling hand to her face. "I didn't mean to lash out at you like that. I don't do that. I don't—"

"Lose control? Fall to pieces? Maybe it would help if you did."

Tess wished she *could* fall apart. She wished she could scream at the injustice and cruelty of a world that would allow this to happen to an innocent child. She wished she could just let go, beat her fists against her chest, tear her hair, do something, *anything,* to give rein to her rage. But losing control wouldn't help Emily, and control was about all Tess had left.

She glanced at Naomi and the hollowness inside her deepened. "How do you do it? After all these years, how do you keep going?"

Naomi glanced away. "Sometimes it might be easier to just give up, to lose all hope. To accept what fate has doled out to me. But then I think about Sadie out there somewhere, wondering if I'm still looking for her, and I make one more phone call. I follow up on that last lead. I do the next interview because if she is still alive, I want her to know that I haven't given up. That I'll never give up."

"I won't give up, either," Tess said fiercely. "But the police *have*."

Naomi squeezed her hand. "I know it seems that way now, but the case will remain open. Leads will be followed. My sister has put a major career change on hold until they find Emily."

Tess lifted her head. "Career change?"

"Abby's applied for acceptance at the FBI Academy, but no matter if she's accepted or not, she's not going anywhere until Emily is found. That's how committed she is." Naomi glanced over her shoulder at the sheriff's station. "They all are, Tess. You have to remain committed, too. There are things you can do on your own to find your daughter, and the Children's Rescue Network can help you.''

"I'll do anything," Tess said brokenly. "You know that."

Naomi nodded. "The first thing is to stay connected with as many of the missing-children's networks and foundations around the country as you can."

There were so many of them, Tess had discovered. Most of them founded in memory of someone's missing child, just like the Children's Rescue Network had been founded in Sadie Cross's memory. A year from now, ten years from now, would such a foundation be Tess's only consolation, her only connection to a daughter she loved more that life itself?

"You'll want to keep Emily's story in the news and her picture in front of the public as much as you can," Naomi said. "And you'll have to find creative ways of doing that now that media interest is waning. You might also want to think about starting a Web site. We can help you with that."

Tess wasn't as proficient on a computer as she should be in this day and age, but she knew about the Internet's power, its ability to reach millions of people in the space of a heartbeat. The rest she would learn.

"What else?"

Naomi paused. "You can go proactive."

"What do you mean?"

"If the note I found is genuine, then the kidnapper has already made contact once, and he was willing to risk detection to do so. You could do another round of television and radio interviews, asking for your daughter's safe return. It's possible the kidnapper will respond to your pleas."

Tess seized on her words. "Then you think the note

was genuine. You don't think it was a hoax as the police seem to.''

"I'm not an expert," Naomi cautioned. "But I can tell you this. For a split second after I found that message, it crossed my mind that it was from Sadie. I know that sounds crazy. She's fifteen years old now, almost a young woman, but I guess a part of me still thinks of her exactly as she was the last time I saw her.'' A shadow darkened her expression, but her eyes were bright and dry. "The point I'm trying to make is that the note touched me in some way. I think a child wrote it.''

Relief welled inside Tess. "I think so, too. I think that child was Emily.''

"If she did write it, then we have to assume she's still alive. And if she's alive, someone may have seen her. A neighbor or a family member of the kidnapper may have suspicions, but for whatever reason, hasn't come forward. You may have to increase the reward offer, and you may also want to consider hiring a private-detective firm to look at the investigation in a different way.''

Tess's heart sank. Immediately after Emily's disappearance, she'd drained her savings to set up a ten-thousand-dollar reward for information pertaining to the kidnapping. That was all the money she had in the world, and her cleaning service had suffered a major financial setback, primarily because she wasn't around to supervise and coordinate the work.

For the last three weeks, she'd haunted the sheriff's station every day, looking for any scrap of information, any bit of news that would give her hope, that would give her confidence the police were doing everything that could be done to find her daughter. She'd worked with the volunteers, stuffing envelopes, answering phones, passing out pictures locally and to the organizations that could distribute them state- and nationwide. No job was too tedious or too overwhelming for her to tackle. She would do anything in her power to bring her daughter home, but Naomi was asking her to do the one thing she could not do. She couldn't raise the reward offer. Not alone.

As if reading her mind, Naomi said sympathetically, "The CRN can set up a fund to help you out financially, but it'll still be expensive. And it could take a while for the donations to mount up. Is there anyone who can help you out immediately?"

Tess shook her head. "Emily and I have no family except for my mother, and she's certainly not a wealthy woman."

"What about Emily's father?"

Tess grew instantly defensive. "What about him?"

"I know he's dead, but what about his family? Could they help?"

"Uh, no," Tess said awkwardly, realizing her initial response must have seemed a little strange. "They're on a fixed income, too. They wouldn't be able to help." Not that his mother would if she could, Tess thought. Mildred Campbell had been dead set against her son's marriage to Tess, and her attitude hadn't softened even when Tess had nursed Alan through the worst of his illness, when she'd kept vigil night and day at his deathbed. The child Tess had been carrying had only served to remind the grief-stricken woman that as one life began another was ending.

And now it was Emily's life on the line.

What about her father?

A shudder racked Tess at the mere thought of her

secret being revealed after all these years. Emily was in grave danger at the hands of her kidnapper, but the note proved she was still alive. She could still be found and rescued.

But if the truth came out now, there might be nothing Tess could do to save her daughter.

Chapter Two

"Here's your mail, Mr. Spencer. And your messages."

Jared Spencer stood gazing out the window of his father's office—his office now—idly gauging the flow of traffic on the street nine stories below. He turned as his secretary bustled into the room. "Thanks, Barbara."

She held up a newspaper. "I brought you a copy of the *Journal,* too. Your father always liked to read the paper first thing in the morning with his coffee." She paused tentatively. "I seem to recall you take yours black."

"You have a good memory."

She turned back to the door. "I'll get you a cup right away."

"No, don't bother," he said, distracted. "I can get my own coffee."

Her eyebrows rose. "It's no trouble."

"That's all right. I don't expect you to wait on me."

"Whatever you say, Mr. Spencer." She fussed with the mail for a moment, then folded the paper just so on his desk. "Oh, dear." Her bifocals hung on a chain around her neck, and she perched them on the end of her nose as she scanned the headlines. "That poor little girl is still missing."

"I beg your pardon?"

She looked up over her glasses. "You haven't heard about it? A five-year-old girl was kidnapped almost three weeks ago from a school playground in Jefferson County. They still haven't found her."

"That's too bad." Jared walked over to his desk and glanced down at the paper. The little girl's picture stared up at him. Dark hair, dark eyes.

"What a beautiful child," he murmured, struck by the girl's arresting features.

"I know. I saw the mother on television the day after it happened. She looked just devastated, poor thing. I have a grandson the same age as the little girl. I kept wondering how I would feel if it was my daughter standing in front of those cameras, begging some madman to bring her child home."

"I hope they find her soon." For a moment, Jared couldn't tear his gaze from the little girl's picture. He hated to think of an innocent child being taken from her mother, suffering unspeakable horrors at the hands of some psycho.

"I hope so, too, but after all this time..." Barbara trailed off, shaking her head. "The world is a sad place. But I guess you know that as well as anyone." Her gray eyes swept the spacious office. "It just doesn't seem the same without him, does it?"

"No, it doesn't."

"Is there anything else I can get you, Mr. Spencer?"

"Not at the moment." He looked up from the newspaper and smiled. "I'm still just trying to get my bearings."

"You'll do fine," she said in a motherly tone. She

paused at the door on her way out and glanced back into the office. "It will be strange, though, without him."

That was an understatement, Jared thought, sorting through his messages. He still hadn't gotten over the shock of his father's sudden death. He kept expecting to look up and see Davis Spencer stroll through the double office doors, demanding to know what the hell Jared was doing sitting behind his desk.

Jared's father had died four weeks ago from a massive coronary that had taken everyone who knew him by surprise. Jared had always thought his father would live forever. He was too stubborn, too powerful, too manipulative to do otherwise, but in the end, he'd been just an ordinary mortal, succumbing to an all-too-human frailty.

And so Jared had been summoned back to the corporate office in Jackson after a six-year stint in New Orleans, where he'd overseen extensive renovations to the grand old Spencer Hotel on Royal Street. The Jackson Spencer, opened at the turn of the century, was the flagship of an elegant fleet of four hotels scattered throughout the South, but the New Orleans Spencer, established some thirty years later, was the most famous, a crown jewel shimmering with old-world ambience and charm in the heart of the Vieux Carré.

The assignment to restore the hotel to its former grandeur had been both challenging and grueling, but it had also been a good place for Jared to make his mark. He'd earned a lot of respect and accolades from his peers over the years, even if at times his drive and determination had made him one of the most hated men in the company. But that, too, had toughened him. At the age of thirty, he'd already become a man to be reckoned with.

Which was a good thing. His younger brother, Royce, had had six years to make inroads in the upper echelons of the Spencer Hotels Corporation while Jared had been out toiling in the trenches. For as long as Jared could remember, he and his brother had been fierce rivals, a situation encouraged by their father to prepare them for the "real" world.

Whether it was on the football field, in the classroom or climbing the corporate ladder, Jared and his brother had been taught at an early age that it was a winner-takes-all world. The loser, it was always understood, got nothing.

But where Jared had thrived on the competition, Royce had grown bitter over the years. He deeply resented Jared's ascension to the presidency of the company, even though the position didn't offer complete autonomy. Jared answered to a powerful board of directors, and his promotion could prove all too temporary if he didn't live up to expectations. His age and experience troubled the old-timers on the board, and they would be watching him closely for any slipups, any lapses in judgment that would give them ample cause to remove him.

Jared didn't know what his brother had to complain about. As executor of a trust set up by their father, Royce had acquired no small amount of power himself.

Frowning, Jared thumbed through the mail. The trust had come as a complete surprise. Unbeknownst to anyone except Davis Spencer and his attorneys, he'd devised the ultimate contest between his sons. The first to produce a Spencer grandchild was given, upon Davis's death, complete control of a fifty-million-dollar trust.

But Royce didn't seem to appreciate the fact that the real prize wasn't the trust, but his family. He had two great kids, a son and a daughter, but unfortunately, he seemed all too preoccupied with the money and the power it brought him. And even that wasn't enough.

"The board should have named me president," he'd ranted after the funeral, when he'd learned of Jared's appointment. "Their decision had nothing to do with who's the better man for the job. You got that appointment solely because you're the eldest. Don't kid yourself into thinking you deserve it. You've been away for six years. *Six years,* damn it, while I stayed here and worked my butt off. While I catered to the old man's every whim."

"What do you think I've been doing down in New Orleans?" Jared retorted. "I paid my dues, too, Royce. I spent fourteen and fifteen hours a day, seven days a week, on that project. You want to talk about working your butt off? You want to talk about sacrifice?"

"Oh, please." Royce gave him a killing look. "You were in New Orleans, for God's sake. Do you know what I would have given to be in your place instead of stuck here with the old man?"

"You could have been there. That project was up for grabs six years ago. But you weren't willing to start out at the bottom, like I was."

"Oh, yeah, it was up for grabs, all right. And you grabbed it so fast, it made my head spin. You just couldn't wait to get down there and prove yourself, could you? You couldn't get out of Mississippi fast enough."

That part was true, Jared thought, but not for the

reasons Royce had mentioned. Jared's leaving had nothing to do with their father and very little to do with ambition. He'd left Mississippi because of Tess.

Tess.

Funny how he hadn't thought of her in years, but the moment he'd returned to Mississippi, the instant he'd smelled the roses at the lake house, her image had popped into his head. He'd been transported back in time, to the very moment when he'd first realized that Tess Granger, the daughter of his mother's house-keeper, had grown into a beautiful, desirable woman.

He was just back from his graduate work at Harvard that summer, home for the first time in nearly two years. The family—including Royce and his new wife—had all driven up to the lake house for the week-end, but by Sunday afternoon, everyone except Jared had gone back to the city. He was finally alone, and the solitude suited him at the time because he'd been feeling pressured by everyone in his life, especially by his father, who insisted it was time for Jared, as the eldest son, to assume his rightful place in the company. And then there was the endless competition with his younger brother—it had all become overwhelming.

Jared had been restless that afternoon, in desperate need of a diversion. And just like that, there she was. A sun-kissed Eve, tempting and beguiling, skinny-dipping in his swimming pool.

Tanned and slim, her golden-brown hair trailing like a mermaid's behind her, she glided through the water like a dream. She didn't have a stitch on, but she seemed completely oblivious to her blatant sexuality.

Who was she? Jared wondered as he watched her from the French doors that looked out on the pool. And what was she doing trespassing on private property?

Not that he cared, of course.

When she turned and floated on her back, he saw that she'd pilfered one of his mother's prized roses and brazenly tucked it behind one ear.

Opening the French door, he stepped out on the patio. She didn't appear to hear him, but floated serenely on the water, eyes closed.

"Hello there."

She gasped, sank, swallowed water, then began to flail wildly. Finally getting her balance, she plunged lower into the water, covering her breasts with her hands. "I...thought everyone was...gone," she managed to sputter.

Jared grinned. "Obviously." He walked over and picked up a towel from one of the patio tables and offered it to her.

It took her a moment to regain her composure, but she did so admirably. She gave him a cool, reproving look. "Turn around, please."

Jared complied. Behind him came the sound of splashing water as she swam to the side and hitched herself out of the pool, then grabbed the towel from his hand.

"You can turn back around now."

Swathed from neck to knee in white terry cloth, she lifted her chin defiantly. "I suppose you're going to tell my mother about this."

"Tell your mother?" How could he, when he didn't know who she was or where she lived? On the Eden side of the lake? Most of the locals did. The north side was reserved for vacation homes and exclusive estates owned mostly by out-of-towners, and was sometimes derisively referred to as Sin City by the locals.

"You don't know who I am, do you?" she challenged.

"Should I?"

"I'm Tess."

"Tess?"

A look of annoyance flickered across her features. "Joelle Granger's daughter. You remember Joelle, don't you? Your *housekeeper?*" She said it almost as a jeer, as if she was chiding him for something other than his faulty memory.

Joelle had served him breakfast on the patio just that very morning, so, of course, Jared remembered her. But he also remembered her daughter as a scrawny kid with wild, curly hair and braces. This couldn't be Tess.

"My God," he said incredulously. "When did you grow up?"

She shrugged. "Oh, let's see, I think it was just after you left for your Ivy League education up north. Harvard, wasn't it? I guess you didn't get back down here to the sticks very often after that. Except for the wild party you threw one New Year's Eve that my mother and I had to clean up after."

He winced at the censure in her tone. "Sorry," he muttered, not knowing exactly what to say in the face of her animosity. "You were paid for your services, weren't you?" He knew it was the wrong thing to say the moment the words left his mouth, and sure enough, her expression darkened.

"Oh, of course. We've always been well paid for our services, Mr. Spencer."

"Call me Jared."

"That wouldn't be appropriate."

"Why not?"

She gave him a withering look. "Because my mother works for you."

"She works for my parents. That doesn't have anything to do with you and me."

"Sure it does." She picked up her clothes.

"Wait," Jared said impulsively. "Don't go yet." He hadn't met a girl he'd found this interesting in ages.

"I have to go. My mother sent me over here to make sure the house was locked up after everyone was gone. But since you're here, you can look after things yourself. You don't need me."

You're wrong, Jared thought. He did need her. He hadn't been a bit lonely until she showed up, but now the prospect of spending the evening alone...without her... "Look. We've obviously gotten off on the wrong foot here. Stay, and let me make it up to you."

"How?"

"We could just hang out for a while. There's no one here but me. I could fix you dinner, wait on you for a change."

Her eyes narrowed. "And what would you expect in return?"

He hesitated a fraction too long. The towel she'd been clutching slipped a bit, and Jared's gaze dipped.

When she saw the direction of his stare, her face flushed bright pink. "In your dreams, buddy."

"Hey," he said to her retreating back. "Aren't you forgetting something?"

She turned at that.

He nodded toward the soggy rose that still clung to her hair. "You've trespassed on private property and stolen one of my mother's prized roses. Serious crimes that usually entail dire repercussions. But if you stay and have dinner with me, we'll just forget all about it."

She gave him a hard, measuring look. "There are two things you need to know about me, Mr. Spencer. One, I don't respond well to threats." She reached up and snatched the rose from her hair, tossing it to the ground at his feet. "But here. By all means, take back the rose. I don't care much for the expensive hybrids anyway. All show and no substance, if you ask me. Like some people I know."

"Ouch." He grinned. "That hurt. What's the second thing I should know about you?"

She gave him a sly smile. "Don't worry about it. You're never going to get close enough to need *that* information." And with that, she disappeared inside the pool house to dress.

As last lines went, it was a good one, and Jared had been left staring after her, intrigued, amused, and aroused as hell.

She'd stolen his heart that day, but it wasn't until the end of the summer that he'd learned what an accomplished thief she truly was.

Scrubbing his face with his hands, he leaned his head back against his chair and closed his eyes. But strangely enough, it wasn't Tess's image that troubled him. It was the little girl's picture in the paper that haunted him. The missing child. For some reason, Jared couldn't get her out of his head.

"WHAT ABOUT THE BANK?" Tess's mother asked at dinner that night. She looked tired tonight, Tess thought. Joelle Granger was still a young woman, not yet fifty, but Emily's disappearance had aged her. The lines in her careworn face had deepened, and her light brown hair had seemed to gray overnight. Like Tess's, her hazel eyes were rimmed with shadows.

She, Tess, and Melanie Kent, Tess's best friend, were seated around her dining-room table, but no one felt like eating, even though the chicken casserole was one of Joelle's specialities.

Tess stared at her plate. Wherever Emily was, had she been given food? Or was she hungry, her little stomach swollen and knotted in pain?

Tess pictured her little girl, weak from hunger, too sick even to cry out...

Overcome by the images, she pushed away her plate. "I'm sorry, Mama, but I can't eat a bite."

"Try to force something down, honey. You can't keep doing this."

"Maybe in a little while." The thought of food made Tess nauseated, so she tried to concentrate on something else. "I went to the bank this afternoon after I talked to Naomi Cross. There's nothing they can do. I don't have enough equity in my house to use as collateral, and there's nothing in the business worth liquidating." Tess's cleaning service had been built primarily on her own blood, sweat and tears, commodities not necessarily valued by a loan institution. "Mr. Cobb was very nice, but as he pointed out, he isn't running a charity organization."

Melanie gasped. Her lovely features contorted in anger. She'd always reminded Tess of a classical painting with her large, lost eyes and brooding mouth. "He didn't say that!"

"Not in so many words, but that was the implication." Tess rubbed her forehead. "I understand their decision. I do. It's business. They can't afford to take on hard-luck cases, but my daughter's life is at stake.

You would think—'' She broke off, shoving back her chair as she began stacking plates.

''Leave the dishes,'' her mother scolded. ''I'll take care of them later.''

''No, Mama, let me do them. I need to keep busy.''

When her mother started to get up, Melanie said quickly, ''Keep your seat, Joelle. I'll help Tess.'' Grabbing the plates, she balanced them in her lap as she deftly guided her wheelchair toward the kitchen.

''You girls don't have to do that,'' Joelle protested. ''I'm perfectly capable of washing my own dishes.''

''You've done more than your share of dishes,'' Melanie insisted, referring to Joelle's long tenure as the Spencers' housekeeper. ''You deserve a little pampering.''

But even though both Joelle and Tess had installed ramps and made their homes as wheelchair accessible as possible after the accident, Joelle's cramped kitchen was still hard for Melanie to navigate. She unloaded the dishes in the sink, then moved back to give Tess room to work.

''I'm just in the way,'' she muttered.

Tess glanced over her shoulder as she started the dish water. ''Stop that. You're never in the way, and you know it. I don't know what I would have done without you these last weeks.''

Melanie bit her lip. ''I just wish I could have done more. I wish I could have prevented this. Oh, Tess, when I think about the way she looked that afternoon—'' She broke off, her blue eyes filling with tears. ''If I'd just waited with her a little longer...''

Melanie was the librarian at Fairhaven Academy, and she always stopped by every afternoon to see Emily before Tess picked her up from school. On that particular day, she'd been one of the last people to see Emily before she disappeared.

Tess sighed. "It's not your fault. You couldn't have known. And besides, there were other teachers on the playground that day. They didn't see anything, either."

"I know, but—"

"But nothing. I meant what I said earlier. I don't know how I would have gotten through this without you."

Melanie's eyes softened. "We've always been there for each other, haven't we?" Melanie's rehabilitation after the accident six years ago had been a long and painful ordeal, but contrary to what she'd said, Tess hadn't been there for her. Not for a long time. And for that, she'd never quite been able to forgive herself.

She forced a smile. "We've been through a lot together, that's for sure."

"Too much," Melanie said with a grimace, tucking her silky blond hair behind one ear.

Tess turned back to the sink, squirted soap into the hot water and began washing the dishes. As she worked, her mind drifted back in time, to the summer her and Melanie's lives had been linked—and changed—forever…

Friends since childhood, Tess had always been the more practical of the two, the more studious, the one who never got into trouble while the impetuous Melanie seemed to hover on the brink of one disaster after another.

So it had come as a surprise to both of them when, in the summer after their junior year in college, Tess had been the one to fall in love, and with a man totally unsuited for her.

Jared Spencer was older, for one thing. More sophisticated. More worldly. Tess sometimes wondered how she had ever let him get under her skin the way he had. He wasn't her type at all. She'd always held nothing but contempt for the southern aristocracy with their customs and attitudes and machinations.

But in spite of her disdain and no small amount of resistance, Jared had finally gotten to her. He'd pursued her arduously and won her over, and sometimes still, in looking back, Tess wondered why he'd been so persistent. Was it a simple case of the forbidden fruit? Had she, the housekeeper's daughter, been an irresistible temptation to rebel against a lifetime of expectations?

Melanie, perhaps not to be outdone, or perhaps because the Spencer charisma had enthralled her, too, had promptly gotten involved with Jared's younger brother, Royce, although she'd kept the relationship a secret. Tess hadn't suspected a thing until she'd opened the door one night, and Melanie had collapsed, hysterical, into her arms.

It wasn't until Tess had finally gotten Melanie to calm down that she noticed the marks on her friend's arms, the telltale discoloration where someone had grabbed her roughly.

Tess stared at the bruises in shock. "Melanie, who did this to you?"

Melanie didn't want to tell her at first, but then finally she whispered, "Royce."

Tess gasped. "Royce Spencer? But you don't even know him!"

Melanie glanced away, unable to meet her friend's gaze. "We've been seeing each other."

"Melanie! He's married!" Tess blurted in horror. In fact, he was practically a newlywed. His sudden marriage had created quite a clamor within the family,

Joelle said, coming as it had after his announcement that he would not pursue an MBA at Harvard, as his brother had done before him, but would instead go directly to work for the Spencer Hotels Corporation.

"I didn't know he was married," Melanie defended. "Not at first. And then when I found out, I was already in love with him. I tried to break it off. I swear I did. I know now what a mistake it was. Tess—" She clutched Tess's arm. "You should have seen the look in his eyes tonight when he grabbed me. I thought he was going to kill me. He was completely out of control."

Tess could hardly comprehend what her friend was telling her. Melanie, involved with a married man? Royce Spencer, capable not only of infidelity, but violence?

In truth, Tess had never cared much for Royce Spencer. He'd always been on the wild side, and just a little too sure that he could get whatever, and whomever, he wanted. He and Tess had had an altercation once at the lake house when he'd made a pass at her. Tess hadn't told her mother about it because she'd handled things herself. She'd slapped Royce's face, he'd laughed and apologized, and for a while, he'd pursued her even harder. But then he'd finally given up, and that had been the end of it.

But this!

"What happened?" she asked.

"I gave him an ultimatum," Melanie said almost defiantly. "I told him if he didn't leave his wife, I'd tell her about us."

"Oh, Mel."

"You hate me," Melanie whispered. "I can see it in your eyes."

"I don't hate you." What Tess felt at the moment was shock. Disbelief. And, yes, more than a little disappointed. Dating a married man—that just wasn't done in her book.

"But you've lost respect for me," Melanie said. "I don't blame you. I don't respect myself much at the moment."

"We'll sort all that out later," Tess murmured, her mind still reeling. "What we have to do now is make sure you're okay. Do you need to see a doctor?"

"He just grabbed me. He didn't…hit me."

"But he threatened you," Tess said. "Maybe we should go to the police."

"No!" Melanie's eyes widened in terror. "Don't you see? No one can know about this. Royce said if I told anyone, he'd kill me. And I believe him. You don't know how dangerous he is—"

"She's right," Tess's mother said from her bedroom doorway.

Both girls spun to face her. Wrapping a white chenille robe tightly around her, Joelle crossed the room to examine the bruises on Melanie's arms. When she finally looked up, her eyes were grave, almost frightened. "No one can find out about this, Tess."

"But he threatened her! We can't let him get away with that!"

Joelle's expression was resolved, worried. "You think the police would believe you? It would be Melanie's word against Royce's, and even if she did manage to convince the authorities she was telling the truth, the family would buy Royce's way out of it. I've watched them get him out of one scrape after another for years, always making excuses for his behavior, always covering up for him. I've been afraid for a long time what that boy might be capable of.''

Tess stared at her, stunned. ''Why didn't you ever say anything?''

''I didn't think I had to,'' Joelle said wearily. ''I hardly ever let you go over to the lake house. I thought all I had to do was keep you away from him. From all of them. And it wasn't hard, because you never seemed to like any of the Spencers anyway.''

''But Jared's different,'' Tess protested. ''He would never hurt anyone.''

Joelle gave her an uneasy glance. ''He may not be like Royce, but he is still a Spencer. It's time you realize what that means, Tess. The Spencers will protect their own, no matter who they have to step on in the process. I want you to stay away from him. Do you hear me?''

''She's right,'' Melanie whispered. ''You have to stay away from the Spencers before something like this happens to you.''

But what none of them had known at that moment, not even Tess, was that she was already irrevocably tied to the Spencers....

Shoving the memories aside, Tess finished the last of the dishes. She dried her hands on a dish towel, then went to kneel beside Melanie. ''I need to talk to you.''

Melanie looked surprised by the urgency in Tess's voice. ''Of course. What is it?''

''I know where I can get the money I need.''

Melanie frowned. ''Where?''

Tess bit her lip. ''Jared's back in Mississippi. I read in the paper that he's been named president of the Spencer Hotels Corporation.'' The article had featured a picture of Jared at a big charity event held at the New

Orleans Spencer. He'd been accompanied by a beautiful redhead with a spectacular figure. His fiancé, the caption had said. Tess hadn't wanted to look at that picture too closely, but somehow she hadn't been able to tear her gaze from it. Jared was getting married. "I'm going to drive to Jackson tomorrow and see him," she told Melanie.

Melanie gripped the arms of her wheelchair. "No!"

"It's the only way, Mel. I have to do this for Emily."

"Emily is precisely the reason why you can't do this!" Melanie's face had gone deathly white. "Have you forgotten why you left town that summer? Why you felt you had to marry Alan Campbell, a man you weren't in love with? Have you forgotten what happened to *me*?"

"I haven't forgotten anything." Tess's gaze dropped to Melanie's wheelchair. "How could I?"

"You can't tell him about Emily. You can't!"

"I know all the reasons why I shouldn't," Tess said quietly. "I know what the dangers are. But what if we're wrong about the kidnapping, Melanie? What if Royce had something to do with Emily's disappearance, and I didn't tell the police about him? What if he has her, and I've kept silent all this time?"

"Tess, listen to me," Melanie said desperately. "You know that's not possible. The police think that whoever kidnapped Sadie Cross ten years ago came back and abducted Emily. Royce had nothing to do with it. But if he finds out about her now, do you think he'd stand by and let that trust slip through his fingers? Even with Emily missing, if he thought you were still a threat to him, he'd come after you in a heartbeat and you know it. He might even come after me, too."

Melanie's pale, thin face hardened with hatred. "Look at me, Tess. Take a good long look. I'm in this wheelchair because I threatened Royce Spencer. He's the one who forced us off the road that night and left us both for dead."

"I know you've always thought that, but the police—"

"Wouldn't even investigate. They never even went out to check Royce's car. It was all swept under the rug, just like it would be now, if you threatened the Spencers. But you thought it was Royce, too, that night, Tess, or else you never would have left town. You would have stayed and fought the Spencers if you hadn't been afraid for your life. And for your baby's life." Melanie cast a glance toward the kitchen door, then lowered her voice so that Joelle wouldn't overhear them. "You burned your bridges by keeping silent, and that took extraordinary courage. Don't get cold feet now. Think of everything you've done to protect your daughter."

It was true. Tess had gone to great lengths to guard her secret, not the least of which had been changing Emily's birth certificate. Alan Campbell had been a medical student before he'd gotten too sick to continue his studies, but he'd still had connections at the hospital in Memphis where he'd trained. He'd had one of his friends who worked in medical records change the entry of Emily's birth from April to August, a full year after Tess had left Eden, as well as the date on all Tess's medical records.

All she'd had to do then was apply for a corrected birth certificate from the state. And since Emily was small for her age, no one had questioned the four-month discrepancy in her development when Tess had returned to Eden two years later. No one knew Emily's true birthday except for Tess, Joelle, Melanie and Emily's pediatrician. And there was no way Royce could get his hands on those records.

"Please, *please,* think about what you're doing," Melanie begged. "You can't tell Jared the truth. You *can't.*" Only one other time had Tess seen the same level of terror in her friend's eyes. "You can't take the chance that Royce would find out. He's still dangerous. He got away with attempted murder back then, and his family helped him. They'd help him now, too, if they had to. For God's sake, don't bring those people back into our lives."

Tess glanced up at her friend. "I'm sorry, but I don't have a choice. They have money and I don't."

"Yes," Melanie said bitterly. "And what if Royce uses his money to make certain Emily stays missing forever? Have you considered that?"

Chapter Three

Secrets have a way of coming back to haunt you, Tess's mother had warned her that summer. As Tess hovered nervously in Jared's office doorway the next day, she felt almost sick with apprehension. The prospect of what she was about to do terrified her.

Melanie was right. The consequences of Tess's actions today could be dire. The threat that had driven her from town—and from Jared's arms—that summer still posed a grave danger. If he refused to help her, she could be risking everything for nothing. She could be putting her daughter in even more jeopardy.

But what choice did she have? What choice had she had six years ago?

Tess swallowed and took a fortifying breath, slowly, deeply, to calm herself, repeating the litany she'd chanted to herself all through the sleepless night. *I'm doing this for Emily.*

Across the room, Jared stood at the window, oblivious to her presence, and for a moment, the urge to slip away before he noticed her was almost overwhelming. But Tess hesitated, her gaze moving over him, drinking in the familiar lines of his body. The wide shoulders.

The narrow waist and slim hips. He was just as tall as she'd remembered, his hair still dark.

In point of fact, Tess had forgotten nothing about Jared Spencer because she still dreamed about him. She still thought about him at night, after Emily had gone to sleep, when the TV was turned off and the house settled into deep silence. Sometimes lying in bed, unable to drift off, Tess would wonder about what might have been, but mostly she thought about what was never meant to be.

She and Jared had come from two very different worlds—his one of wealth and privilege, hers one of hard work and sacrifice. Still, it might have worked, they might have made it work, if it hadn't been for a series of events that summer that had changed Tess's life—and Melanie's—forever. The night Melanie had showed up at Tess's door had only been a portent.

But Jared had loved her once, Tess thought, her eyes misting. He'd once promised her there wasn't anything he wouldn't do for her.

Would he feel that way now when he found out the truth...?

"Promise me," Tess whispered as she and Jared lay on his boat, watching the stars turn on one by one in an indigo sky. They were alone on the lake, drifting aimlessly, neither of them anxious to return to shore. To reality. "Promise you won't say anything until I'm ready."

Jared rolled to his side and propped himself on his elbow, gazing down at her. "They're going to find out about us sooner or later, Tess. They may even already know." He trailed a finger down her bare stomach, making her shiver. "Why are you so afraid?"

"You know why. I'm not the sort of girl your parents would want to see you bring home. They won't approve of me and you know it."

He hesitated, frowning. "They will in time."

"But what if they don't? What if my mother loses her job?"

"You think she'd get fired because of us? I wouldn't let that happen."

"Maybe you couldn't stop it. Maybe they'd kick you out, too."

"I'm not a kid, Tess. I've got my own place. I'm not exactly worried about being homeless."

"But you're destined to take over the company someday. It's what you want. Your father could force you out because of me."

"Stop borrowing trouble. That's not going to happen, either."

He was trying to reassure her, but Tess longed to hear him say that he didn't care if it did happen. He could be happy without the Spencer money, without the prestige and power, so long as he had her.

But he didn't say it, and Tess was afraid his silence spoke volumes.

She closed her eyes as his fingers whispered along her skin, barely touching her and yet eliciting a response so needy, so primal, she hardly recognized herself. This wasn't supposed to happen. Not to her. She was too levelheaded. And she didn't even like the Spencers.

But Jared was different. He always had been, and Tess was only now starting to admit to herself that she'd nursed secret feelings for him for years. Maybe that was why she was so reluctant to bring their relationship out into the open. Jared Spencer was a fantasy come true. She didn't want reality screwing up everything. When his family found out about them…*if* they made him choose…

Tess shivered, and Jared pulled her even closer.

"I've got an idea," he murmured.

"What?"

"My family's having a celebration here at the lake next week. It's my parents' anniversary. I want you to come as my date. Maybe once you get to know us, you'll realize we aren't the monsters you seem to think we are."

"I can't," Tess said in alarm. "My mother has to work that night, and I promised I'd help her."

Jared rolled to his back and stared at the sky. "You don't have to do that."

"Why not?" she challenged. "I'm not ashamed of what my mother does for a living. If it's good enough for her, it's good enough for me."

"Still wearing that chip on your shoulder, Tess? Still think you've got something to prove?"

"It's not that." She drew her knees into her chest and wrapped her arms around her legs. "I just want you to see me for who I really am. Don't expect me to change just because of us."

"Then why should I have to change?"

"I never said you did."

"Not in so many words, but there's always this underlying tension when we're together," he said. "I always feel as if I have to make excuses for who I am and for what my family has. You put up defenses that I don't know how to break through."

"If I'm so much trouble, why do you even bother?" she asked, stung by his words.

"Because no matter how hard you try to push me away, I can't stop thinking about you." He tugged her down beside him, holding her close, discarding her bathing-suit top in one fluid motion. "I can't stop wanting you," he whispered.

The night air swept over Tess, cooling her, drawing an inevitable response. But Jared was there to keep her warm. Jared was there to cover her nakedness with his, making her want him so badly Tess could hardly believe that just a few short weeks ago, she'd never been with a man, never experienced the intense pleasure of lovemaking.

But Jared had changed all that.

He kissed her deeply, making her melt in his arms. Making her sigh his name.

"Meet me," he whispered in her ear.

"When? Where?"

"I'm going to New Orleans tomorrow, but I'll be back next week for the party. Meet me down by the lake after dinner. I can't spend the whole evening under the same roof with you and not touch you."

"Touch me now," she begged.

And he did. Over and over....

As the memories spun away, Tess saw that Jared had turned from the window and was staring at her. Her face flushed hot, and she braced herself for his reaction. Her mouth dry, the muscles in her throat taut and aching, she stared back at him. And for the life of her, she couldn't think of a single thing to say.

But it didn't matter because his first words said it all.

"May I help you?" he asked in a tone that held not the slightest note of recognition.

THE YOUNG WOMAN who stood in his doorway looked as if she might turn and bolt at any second. When Jared started across the room toward her, she did exactly that.

"Wait!"

She hesitated, glancing over her shoulder. Uncertainty flickered in her eyes.

"Are you lost?" When she didn't answer immediately, he said, "Whose office are you trying to find? Maybe I can help you."

Resentment flashed in her hazel eyes. "I'm not lost. I came here to see you."

"Do we have an appointment?"

"No." Her chin lifted. "I slipped passed the receptionist in the lobby. And your secretary wasn't at her desk."

He cocked his head slightly, studying her. "Do I know you?"

"I'm Tess," she said, and now it was annoyance that settled over her features, precisely the way it had six years ago when he'd failed to recognize her.

Stunned, Jared could only stare at her. Back then her transformation from a gangly teenager to a striking young woman had taken him by surprise, but this new metamorphosis was even more shocking. And disturbing.

He wouldn't have recognized her. Not in a million years. Her face was pale and drawn, with dark circles underneath her eyes and deep pain within. And she was so thin! Not fashionably slender, but skin and bones, as if she'd been sick recently and hadn't completely recovered. She wore a slim, dark skirt and white, sleeveless blouse, but the elegant lines of her clothing did little more than hint at the curves she'd once had. The curves he still remembered so well.

She'd pinned up her hair, taming the curls that used

to cascade down her back so freely. Gone was the luster, the golden highlights that had glinted like fire in
the sunlight. He'd always loved Tess's hair, Jared
thought with a stab of regret he didn't want to analyze
too closely.

It was he who stood speechless now.

She took a tentative step inside his office. "If you
have a moment, I'd like to speak with you."

At least her voice hadn't changed. It was low and
slightly husky, not as overtly sexy as Demi Moore's or
Kathleen Turner's but close. When she'd used that
voice to whisper to him, to tell him how much she
loved him, how much she wanted him...

It had been a lie, of course. She'd played him for a
fool that summer, and he would be crazy if he gave
her anything more than the time of day.

He glanced at his watch and frowned. "I have a
meeting in fifteen minutes. I can spare you ten of
those."

Some of the old resentment flashed again in her eyes,
but something else, another emotion he couldn't quite
define, subdued it. She nodded and walked into his
office.

He motioned for her to take a seat and he moved
around his desk, putting the heavy expanse of granite
between them. "So what can I do for you?"

"First, let me say, I heard about your father, and I'm
sorry."

"Thanks," Jared said curtly. He wished he could
take some satisfaction in the pain he saw in her face,
but he couldn't. Not even after what she'd done.

"So this is all yours now," she said softly, glancing
around the commodious office. Her gaze came back to
his. "Just the way it was always meant to be."

He shrugged. "Somehow I don't think you came here to congratulate me."

Regret flickered in her eyes. Regret for what she'd done? For what she'd thrown away?

She placed her purse in her lap, the fingers of her right hand moving back and forth over the clasp, squeezing and releasing, squeezing and releasing. She was obviously nervous. Jared couldn't imagine what she had to say to him after all these years. And though he had a good deal he'd like to say to her, he held his tongue.

"I realize you're a busy man, so I'll get right to the point." Her chin lifted slightly. "I need money. A lot of it."

He schooled his outward reaction, but inside, Jared was astounded. Tess Granger was the last person he would have expected to come asking for money. Six years ago, she'd worn her pride like a shield, against him, against his family. Against the whole world, he sometimes thought.

And now here she was, with her hand out.

"That's a little ironic, don't you think? That you would come here, of all places."

Color tinged her pale cheeks. "This isn't easy for me. Believe me, if there'd been any other way…" She trailed off, closing her eyes for a moment. "But I thought…we were close once—"

He cut her off. "Do yourself a favor, Tess. Don't go there."

The flush deepened, but anger glinted in her eyes. "All right," she said in a grim, determined voice. "I'll put it as simply as I can. My daughter is missing, and I need money to get her back."

"Your daughter?" Jared's gaze dropped to her left

hand. She wore a thin, gold band around her third finger. "You're married?"

"I was." Her gaze met his without wavering. "My husband died a few years ago. I have a five-year-old daughter named Emily. Almost three weeks ago, she was kidnapped from a school playground. We don't know by whom or where she was taken. The police have—"

"Wait a minute." Jared picked up the newspaper from his desk and opened it to the picture of the missing child. For some reason, he hadn't been able to toss the paper out. "Is this your daughter?"

Tess's face grew even paler as she stared at the photograph. "Yes. That's Emily."

Jared turned the paper so that he could study the picture. He was struck, as he had been yesterday, by the extraordinary beauty of the child. In spite of her dark hair and eyes, she looked a lot like Tess, although he hadn't made the connection before, at least not consciously. But now he could even see that same damnable pride in the way the little girl held her chin, that same glow of defiance emanating from her brown eyes. And also like Tess, there was something exquisitely vulnerable about the child, something that brought out a protective instinct in Jared he never even knew he possessed. The thought of someone taking that innocent little girl, harming her—

He glanced up at Tess. "I'm sorry. I've only been back in Mississippi a few days. I've been living in New Orleans for the past six years."

"Yes, I know. I...heard," she stammered, as if not wanting to reveal how she'd come by the information. Had she been asking about him? Keeping tabs on him?

Jared was hard-pressed to believe it considering their final conversation.

"I heard about the kidnapping, but I never dreamed the victim was your daughter." He got up and moved around the desk to stand in front of her. "What happened?"

Tess's eyes filled with tears, and for a moment she struggled for composure, putting a hand to her mouth as if to suppress her emotions.

No matter how much he'd hardened his heart during the past six years, Jared couldn't resist that. She was so obviously a woman in agony. A woman who desperately needed help. He sat down beside her, not taking her hand, but finding that he wanted to.

"What happened?" he asked again.

She drew a quivering breath and turned to face him. "I don't know how much you remember about Eden, but Emily was kidnapped from the playground at Fairhaven Academy, a private school on the north side of town. Do you remember it?"

"A big, ivy-covered building, manicured grounds?"

Tess nodded, and Jared wondered if she had any idea that she'd just presented him another irony. Tess Granger, a fierce and proud member of the proletariat, sent her child to a private school, just as the Spencers had done for generations. Just as she'd once ridiculed them for doing. *"Don't try to change me,"* she'd warned him over and over. He'd never tried to change her. All he'd ever wanted to do was love her, but that hadn't been enough, he thought with an edge of bitterness.

"When I went to pick her up that afternoon, the teachers couldn't find her. She'd been with a group of her classmates on the playground, but no one saw her wander off. No one saw anything. No cars, no strangers, nothing. It was as if she vanished into thin air.''

"The little girl who disappeared a long time ago,'' Jared mused. "She went to Fairhaven, too, didn't she?''

Tess nodded. "Her name was Sadie Cross. No trace of her was ever found. Emily disappeared on the anniversary of Sadie's abduction.''

A chill crawled up Jared's backbone. "What do the police make of that?''

"They think there's a connection. Not only did Emily disappear on the anniversary of the abduction, but she also bears a resemblance to Sadie. Both have dark hair and brown eyes.'' Her gaze settled briefly on Jared's face before she glanced away again, as if she couldn't quite meet his eyes. "A profiler was brought in. He thought that Sadie's abductor might have taken her to replace someone in her life, a child who had died perhaps, and that ten years later, Emily might have been taken to replace Sadie.''

The chill inside Jared deepened. He had a sudden vision of the lake, of the secrets that could be hidden below the crystalline waters. "Is it possible that Emily was taken on the anniversary of Sadie's disappearance just to throw off the police?''

She looked almost stricken by the idea. "I…guess it's possible. The police have no real leads, no evidence, no clues except for a note that was found on a car in my driveway.''

"A ransom note?''

"No, a note from a child that said…she'll be home soon. The police think it could be a hoax, but I know it was a message from Emily. I know she's still alive, but the police have given up on her.''

"What do you mean, the police have given up on her?" Jared said with a frown.

"They've scaled down the search. Hundreds of volunteers came from all over the state to help in the initial ground search, but now, after so much time has passed…Emily could be anywhere." Tess wiped a tear from the corner of her eye. "But I don't care where she is. I don't care what I have to do to find her. I'm not giving up. I'll never give up."

She was so close and she seemed so frail, so distraught. The desire to touch her was so strong that Jared rose and strode over to the window, putting distance between them. "You said you needed money."

"I've offered a ten-thousand-dollar reward for information leading to her whereabouts, but that may not be enough. And I want to hire a private investigator, especially now that the police have cut back on their search. All that takes money, and I don't have any," she said simply. Once, there might have been a spark of defiance in her tone, but now she merely sounded… desperate.

Jared turned to face her. "How much do you need?"

She bit her lip. "I've been told the reward should be at least fifty thousand dollars. I don't have any idea how much a private investigator will cost."

He walked over to his desk, sat down, and pulled out his checkbook. "Do you have anyone in mind?" When she shook her head, he said, "We've used a firm here in Jackson on occasion. The guy in charge knows his stuff. I'll be happy to give you his number."

"Thank you."

Jared filled in the check, scribbled his name, then handed it across the desk to her.

Her gaze lifted to his. "Just like that? No…questions

asked?'' The intense relief in her eyes was almost painful to witness.

"Your child is missing," he said grimly. "I think that pretty much answers all my questions." He nodded toward the check. "Will that be enough to start?"

She glanced at the amount and gasped. "I didn't mean…that's too much…"

"You said you didn't know how much it would take. Will that get you started?"

She seemed overcome by emotion. "I don't know how to thank you," she finally managed to say. "I'll pay you back. Every cent of it, no matter how long it takes me."

He held up a hand in protest. "Don't worry about that now. Just find your daughter. Will you keep me posted?"

Fear flickered across her features. "There's one other thing."

"Yes?"

She glanced down at the check in her hand. "I don't know how to say this after you've been so generous."

"Just say it."

"Could this remain confidential?"

Annoyance darted through him. "If you think I'm going to issue a statement to the press—"

"That's not what I meant," she cut in. "I'd…rather your family not know."

He gave her an exasperated look. "They're not the ogres you've always made them out to be, Tess. Do you really think any one of them would have refused to help if you'd come to them? Even after what you did that night—"

Tess rose swiftly, as if she suddenly couldn't wait to get out of his office. "Just promise me."

"You've always been one for extracting a lot of promises, but it seems to me you've never been that great at keeping them."

She gave him a hard, brittle look. "Only when I had good reason not to."

"Is that so?" He stood and walked around the desk to face her. She still looked as if she wanted to flee, but to make sure she didn't, he reached out and took her arm. Awareness shot through him. "Why did you do it, Tess?"

"What does it matter?" she asked. "It was a long time ago."

"Really? Because it seems like yesterday to me."

"Jared—"

It was the first time he'd heard her say his name in six years, and he couldn't help but respond. The throaty quality of her voice…the way she gazed up at him…

"Just tell me why," he said almost savagely.

A hint of the old rebellion glinted in her eyes. "I don't want to talk about that night. What's the point?"

"The point is—" He drew her slightly toward him. "You took something valuable that night, Tess. Something that didn't belong to you. And then you just walked away. I'm not letting you leave here until you tell me why."

Chapter Four

Because your brother wanted me dead, Tess almost blurted.

She caught herself in time. She couldn't tell Jared about the conversation she'd overheard that night between Royce and his wife, Ariel. She couldn't tell him about the accident that had left her best friend in a wheelchair, because Royce Spencer was still a threat. His motives for wanting Tess and her daughter out of the way were as strong as ever.

He had his own children now, Tess had read somewhere. A boy and a girl. The perfect family. But Emily would always remain the first Spencer grandchild. The heir to a secret trust that only a handful of people had known about until Davis Spencer's death.

And that was why Tess had left town. That was why she'd married Alan Campbell, a young man who had been just as lonely and scared as she was that summer. Alan had given Tess his name so that Emily could be born a Campbell. And in return, Tess had watched over him, remained by his side until he'd succumbed to the AIDS-related disease that had ravaged him.

But she could tell Jared none of that.

She shouldn't have come here, Tess thought in despair. She should have found another way to get the money instead of opening up all these old wounds. She'd long ago resigned herself to the fact that she and Jared were never meant to be, but she'd taken comfort in the knowledge that she'd done the right thing back then. She had Emily, and they were both safe.

But her daughter was no longer safe. Emily was missing, and in order to save her, Tess had willingly walked back into a den of lions.

A shudder ripped through her as she thought back to that night. As she remembered the fear and desperation that had driven her from Jared's arms....

"Tess, I swear. I've never seen you like this. You're as nervous as a cat," her mother scolded. "What's wrong with you?"

They were standing in the spacious kitchen in the Spencers' lake house, preparing for the anniversary celebration. Though it was to be a small, intimate affair, a caterer had been brought in from the city to prepare the meal, but it was Joelle's job to keep everything running smoothly. And since the caterer had arrived shorthanded, Tess had been pressed into serving.

She'd grown more nervous as the evening wore on. What if she spilled something—the three-thousand-dollar bottle of wine Davis Spencer had purchased at an auction to much fanfare and publicity—all down the front of Cressida Spencer's white gown?

"Sorry, Mama," Tess muttered as she righted a crystal champagne flute she'd almost toppled. "I'll try to be more careful."

Joelle frowned at her. "Is something wrong, honey? You look a little pale, and you haven't been yourself for days. Are you coming down with the summer flu?"

"I'm fine, Mama. Just a little tired."

But it was more than that. Tess's period was almost a week late, and she was never late. She tried to tell herself it was just stress, but what if she really was pregnant?

I can't be, she thought desperately. She and Jared had been so careful. They'd always used protection. And they hadn't been together that many times anyway.

It only takes once, a little voice taunted Tess.

"What are you going to do?" Melanie had asked Tess earlier when she'd driven Tess out to the lake house.

"I'll have to tell Jared," she said.

"What if he wants you to get rid of the baby?"

Tess had recoiled in horror. "He wouldn't!"

"What do you think he's going to do, Tess? Marry you? Spencers don't marry ordinary people like us. They find ways to get rid of us."

Trying to block out her friend's warning, Tess whirled back to the counter, away from her mother's suspicious scrutiny. But the sudden movement brought on a wave of dizziness. As Tess grabbed for the counter to steady herself, her hand hit one of the goblets, knocking it to the floor. French crystal shattered against African slate.

Horrified, Tess dropped to her knees and began picking up the shards.

"I hope you realize that glass was Lalique," said a cool voice above her.

Tess looked up, dreading to see who stood over her. The white silk dress came into focus first, then the diamonds around her wrist, then Cressida Spencer's smooth, lovely features. Tess's heart began to pound.

In truth, she'd always been a little frightened of Jared's tall, blond mother.

"I'm...sorry," Tess stammered.

Icy blue eyes glared down at her. "As well you should be. Those champagne flutes have been in my husband's family for generations. They're priceless. I had them sent up here especially for our anniversary because they mean so much to me. They've weathered hurricanes, tornadoes, and a fire that almost destroyed everything else in the house. And now because of your carelessness—"

"It was my fault." Joelle stepped quickly between Tess and Cressida Spencer. "You can take it out of my salary." Next to Cressida, Tess's mother seemed diminished, faded, and that made Tess angry.

"I just said they were priceless," Cressida snapped. "Neither of you will see enough money in your lifetime to replace that set."

Everyone in the kitchen, including the caterers, had stopped to watch the tableau. The room fell almost deathly silent.

"If you want to blame someone, blame me," Tess said, rising to her feet. As intimidated as she was by Cressida Spencer, she wasn't about to let her mother be faulted for something she'd done. "I knocked the glass off the counter. It was an accident."

"It's inconsequential to me who was at fault. The glass is still broken." Cressida gestured impatiently at the floor, and as she did so, her bracelet slid from her wrist, landing with an ominous clatter among the shards of glass.

Cressida uttered a sharp oath. "I had that clasp repaired only a month ago!" She waited for someone to retrieve the bracelet for her.

Tess bent and picked it up, handing it back with the utmost care. She'd never seen such brilliant diamonds, such a magnificent piece of jewelry. But for some reason, the glittering gemstones left her cold. Like Cressida, herself.

Cressida's gaze narrowed on Tess as her hand closed possessively over the bracelet. "You're Tess, aren't you?"

Something in her eyes made a chill go through Tess. "Yes."

"You've changed since the last time I saw you." She gave Tess a cool critique. "You've gotten taller, prettier. But I've always thought your mother should make you do something about all that hair. It's not at all becoming."

She couldn't have said anything more hurtful if she'd tried. Tess's long hair had always been a point of pride with both her and her mother. Joelle called it her crowning glory.

"Promise me you'll never cut those beautiful curls, Tessie," she would say when Tess was little.

"I won't, Mama. I'll let it grow as long as Rapunzel's."

And now, because of Cressida Spencer, Tess had an urgent desire to rush out and chop it all off. Every last curl.

Her gaze lifted to Cressida's, and she saw the glint of malice in the blue eyes, a hint of a satisfied smile. Suddenly it occurred to Tess that Cressida knew about her and Jared, and that was why she'd made the disparaging remark. Not because she was upset about the glass, but to put Tess in her place.

Cressida turned and walked serenely from the room, leaving Tess trembling in anger. But when she would have gone after her, Joelle grabbed her arm. "Don't do it, Tess."

"But, Mama—"

"Don't make trouble. I need this job." Since Tess's father had died when she was ten, Joelle had had a hard time making ends meet. Tess didn't want to make things even more difficult for her.

She acquiesced for her mother's sake, but the look in Cressida's eyes had told Tess what she'd always suspected. What Melanie had warned her about. She would never be accepted by the Spencers.

Thankfully, the rest of the evening passed more smoothly. Tess managed to execute her serving duties without incident, although she could feel Cressida's disapproving gaze on her as she moved about the room.

And then there was Jared's gaze, the exact opposite of his mother's. Tess tried to keep her own eyes averted because every time she looked at him, every time she caught his smile, she went hot and cold all over. She hadn't seen him in almost a week, and she couldn't wait to be in his arms again. But would he still want her when she told him about the baby?

Jared's baby.

A tiny thrill raced through her at the thought.

He caught her coming out of the kitchen when no one was around, and he grabbed her around the waist, pulling her toward him for a long, slow kiss.

"Someone will see us!" she protested, trying to push him away. But it was only a token resistance, and they both knew it. He was irresistible in his tuxedo.

He laughed and pulled her even closer. "Let them see us. I don't care."

"Well, I do! Your mother is already mad at me because I broke one of her champagne glasses."

"She'll get over it. She has hundreds of glasses."

"But this was part of a set that's been in your family for generations. She said it was priceless, and I ruined it," Tess said forlornly.

Jared shrugged. "Accidents happen. Forget it."

"I can't. I think she blames my mother for it."

"I'll talk to her, okay? It's no big deal."

Tess started to tell him it was a very big deal if his mother didn't like her, especially in light of what she had to tell him later. But once his lips touched hers, everything else faded. She clung to him for a long moment, savoring the feel of his body against hers, relishing the promises he whispered in her ear.

"I don't know how much longer the party will drag on," he murmured against her lips. "I'll try to get away by midnight. If you're not down by the lake by then, I'll come and find you."

She drew away. "Promise?"

"Of course." But there was a look in his brown eyes, a flash of doubt, that seemed a portent of things to come.

But as it turned out, Tess was able to slip away long before midnight. The wind off the water had picked up during the evening, carrying occasional drops of rain. She pulled on her windbreaker as she followed the path through the woods. In spite of the coming storm, the moon was up, a great, silvery orb trimmed around the edges with dark, lacy clouds.

The path led straight to the boathouse, and as Tess rounded the side, she saw that someone stood at the end of the dock. She started to call out, but then she realized the man wasn't Jared. It was Royce, and he wasn't alone. A woman stood facing him, and Tess saw in the moonlight that it was his wife. Had they slipped down here for a private moment? she wondered. They were newlyweds, after all, in spite of the fact that he'd been carrying on with Melanie.

Glancing around, Tess hoped to retrace her steps without being detected. She had no wish to intrude on their privacy. Besides, if she came face-to-face with Royce Spencer, the temptation to tell him exactly what she thought of him might prove too great.

"What the hell was so important that you had to drag me all the way down here?" he demanded. "In case you haven't noticed, it's about to rain, Ariel."

"I don't care. I want to know why you're so worried about Tess Granger. You said something earlier about taking care of her. I want to know what you meant."

Tess froze. A moment ago, she'd wanted to retreat, but now she melted into the shadows of the boathouse, her heart hammering in her chest.

Like Jared, Royce was dressed in a tux. He was tall and slender, with the kind of handsome features women seemed drawn to. But there was something else about him, an attitude, an arrogant restlessness that gave Tess the impression he was constantly on the prowl for trouble. And that whatever trouble came his way, he could not only handle, but would probably get away with. And like all the Spencers, he exuded an air of self-confidence and good breeding.

In contrast, Ariel Spencer was slight, dark and non-descript, a woman easily overpowered by her husband. Tess wondered fleetingly if that was why Royce had married her.

He spoke softly, but there was an unpleasant edge to his voice. "She and Jared have been going at it hot and heavy all summer. They think they've been discreet, but I found out about them through...a friend.

And it's a good thing I did. I'll be damned if I let some gold-digging little nothing mess up my plans.''

''Is that really why you're so bothered?'' The wind whipped Ariel's long, dark hair across her face, and she peeled it back with an almost frantic movement of her hand.

''What do you mean?''

''I mean, I've seen the way you look at her. I can't help wondering if the reason you're so upset is because she's seeing Jared instead of you.''

Royce gave a sharp bark of laughter. ''You're joking, right? You think I'd give someone like her a second look? She's the housekeeper's daughter, for God's sake.''

''Don't pretend you're so discriminating.'' Ariel's voice oozed resentment.

Royce scowled down at her. ''What the hell is that supposed to mean?''

''Blond hair, blue eyes, about so tall.'' She measured several inches above her own head. ''Sound familiar?''

''Not especially.''

''I saw you,'' Ariel said through gritted teeth. ''Earlier tonight, in this very spot. The two of you were arguing. Are you going to stand there and deny it?''

Tess hadn't so much as moved a muscle. She stood in the shadows of the boathouse, a chill racing up and down her spine. Melanie had blond hair and blue eyes. And she'd been here earlier, dropping Tess off. Had she stayed and talked to Royce? But why would she, after the way he'd threatened her?

''You don't know what you saw,'' he said in disgust.

''You're denying that you made plans to meet her here later?''

''Of course I'm denying it. It was just someone asking for directions.'' He started to move past her, but Ariel grabbed his arm.

''I'm warning you, Royce. I won't let you make a fool of me. If I find out you're cheating on me, I'll go straight to your father and tell him everything.''

''You'll do nothing of the sort. You'll keep your mouth shut, that's what you'll do.'' The anger in his voice was sharpened now by something darker, more menacing.

Ariel flung her head back. ''Why should I?''

His nostrils flared as he gazed down at her. ''Because you have as much at stake here as I do. You go to my father, and I'll go straight to the police in Oxford.''

Ariel gasped, her hand flying to her heart. ''You wouldn't!''

''Don't test me, Ariel. I'll do whatever I have to do to win. You should know that by now.'' He made a slight movement toward her, and she stepped back quickly, as if she was afraid of him. ''I held up my end of the bargain. I expect you to do the same. You're a loving, dutiful wife. Start acting like it.''

Ariel's voice trembled when she spoke. ''Maybe I would if you'd be the kind of husband you promised to be.''

''Meaning?''

''Why can't you look at me the way you look at Tess Granger?''

''Her again? You have a one-track mind. How many times do I have to tell you, my interest in Tess Granger is purely financial. If you've seen me looking at her, it's because I'm trying to figure out how to keep her from getting her money-grubbing hands on that trust.''

Tess could still see him in the moonlight, and her

blood ran cold at the look on his face, the hardness in his eyes. She had no idea what he was talking about, but she instantly remembered every single word her mother and Melanie had said about him. And in that moment, seeing his face, Tess believed them.

"But she can't know about the trust," Ariel said. "You told me that Jared doesn't even know."

"I don't think she does know about it," Royce said. "She's just after Spencer money. Any Spencer money. Although who's to say that some stupid little clerk in my father's attorney's office didn't spill the beans to her? After all, that's how I found out."

"And the moment you did, you drove straight up to Oxford and persuaded me to marry you," Ariel said bitterly. "You insisted we elope, when you knew how much I wanted a church wedding."

"So what? When you heard my proposition, you were as eager as I was to tie the knot."

Ariel wrapped her arms around her middle, as if she suddenly felt chilled in the damp air. "Maybe I was eager because I was in love with you."

"That's your problem. Love was never part of the bargain."

"How can you be so cold?"

"Oh, come on. Don't go all self-righteous on me. Your hands aren't exactly clean in all this. DUI is a serious offense. One of those kids in the other car damn near died. You'd be in jail right now if it wasn't for me."

"That's not true. Daddy never would have let it come to that."

"It's all 'Daddy' can do to keep himself out of the gutter these days. Which is exactly why you had no problem accepting my proposition."

Ariel raised her hand to slap him, but Royce caught her wrist, bending her hand back until she cried out. Almost against her will, Tess started forward, but Royce released Ariel and moved away from her. "Don't ever try that again."

"What would you do—kill me?" she taunted.

His laugh was low and sinister. "I don't think you want to find that out."

Tess hadn't imagined the edge in his voice, the warning in his stance. This was the same Royce Spencer who had threatened Melanie. The same Royce Spencer who, although Tess still didn't understand why, had it in for her.

She'd heard somewhere, in one of her psychology classes perhaps, that people with sociopathic tendencies were often perceived as good-looking and personable. Charming, even. That's how they conned their victims into trusting them. Was Royce Spencer a sociopath?

Tess closed her eyes. No wonder Melanie had been so terrified of him that night. No wonder his own wife seemed afraid of him now. Royce Spencer was a very dangerous man.

"It was the way you were raised," Ariel said in a strangely subdued voice. "That's why you're like this. How can any father pit his sons against one another the way he has?"

"Not that I have to defend him to you, but everything he did taught us a valuable lesson, unlike the lessons your old man taught you. We learned at any early age that the losers of this world get nothing. Jared's always been a master at playing the good son. He's always had the old man eating out of his hand, but he's made one fatal mistake. He's underestimated me. They both have. I've got something Jared will never have. The killer instinct. The willingness to do whatever it takes to win. And that trust is the ultimate contest.''

''The son who presents Davis Spencer with the first grandchild gets control of fifty million dollars,'' Ariel said, still in that restrained tone. ''Which is where I come in.''

''That's right. By the time I get Tess Granger out of the picture, you'd better be pregnant.''

''What are you going to do to her?''

He hesitated, then shrugged. ''I guess I can tell you. I may need you to back me up.'' He glanced at his watch. ''Sometime tonight, before everyone leaves, Mother will discover that her diamond bracelet is missing. When she sounds the alarm, someone from the caterer's staff will reluctantly come forward and swear she saw Tess take it. The old man will be livid. He'll call the police, and off to jail our little Tess goes. If Jared tries to intervene, so much the better. Let's see how he fares in the old man's eyes when he tries to defend a thief.''

''You've got it all figured out, don't you?'' Ariel said.

''I don't like to pat myself on the back, but by the time I'm through with Tess Granger, nobody will believe her, not even Jared. And better yet, she could be facing a five-to-ten-year prison sentence.''

''And you'll see that she gets it, too, won't you?'' Ariel rubbed her arms with her hands. ''I wouldn't want to be in her shoes.''

Royce laughed again.

''Aren't you forgetting something?'' Ariel asked softly. ''If they've been seeing each other all summer, it's possible she could already be pregnant.''

Royce was facing Tess now, and she could have sworn he looked directly at her in the shadows. Then his expression turned dark. "Well, in that case, I'd have to find a more permanent solution, wouldn't I? One that would take care of the kid, too."

Hardly daring to even breathe, Tess waited as they spoke for several more minutes. Then Royce headed back up the path toward the house, and Ariel lingered on the dock, gazing down into the water.

Raising her head, Ariel stared at the spot where Royce had disappeared into the woods, and in the moonlight, her face appeared oddly serene. She waited a moment, then hurried up the path behind him.

Tess's legs almost buckled. She leaned heavily against the wall of the boathouse, contemplating everything she'd just heard. Because of some trust, Royce Spencer was going to try to frame her.

She put her hands to her face, trying to make sense of it all. Why was she such a threat to Royce Spencer? What could she possibly have to do with a trust set up by his father?

Something Ariel said came back to her. "The son who presents Davis Spencer with the first grandchild gets control of fifty million dollars."

Her hand crept to her stomach. What if she really was pregnant? What if at this very moment she was carrying Jared's child? The first Spencer grandchild?

The idea of a pregnancy had terrified Tess earlier. She'd worried all day about how Jared would react, what her mother would say, what everyone in town would think. Now all she cared about was what Royce Spencer would do to her. And to the baby.

And with that thought, a fierce protective instinct, like nothing Tess had ever experienced before, rose inside her. She wouldn't let anyone harm her baby. Not Royce Spencer. Not anyone.

She glanced around frantically in the darkness. But what should she do? What *could* she do? Run to Jared? Would he believe her? Would he be able to help her?

But what if the bracelet was discovered missing before she got to Jared? What if she was taken to jail before she had a chance to explain? Would he believe anything she said after that?

For now, there was only one thing she could do. The only way she could protect herself was to get away from here as quickly as possible.

It was drizzling by the time she started up the path, and she pulled her windbreaker tightly around her as she ran through the wet darkness.

Blind with fear and panic, she didn't see the shadow on the trail in front of her until it was too late. A scream rose to her throat.

Melanie put out her hands and caught Tess's arms. "Tess? What are you doing out here?"

"Oh my God, Melanie." Tess was shaking so badly she could hardly speak. "Thank God, it's you. I thought you were Royce—"

"Royce?" Melanie glanced anxiously over Tess's shoulder. "You saw him? He's down here?"

"He was earlier, but he went back up to the house." She clutched Melanie's arms. "You have to help me. I have to get out of here."

"What's wrong? What happened?"

"He's trying to set me up. He wants to get rid of me. Melanie, please. You have to help me get out of here."

Her desperation must have gotten through, because

Melanie grabbed her arm. "Come on. I left my car up on the road."

Tess allowed Melanie to pull her along the wet path to the road. Only then, when they were safely inside, did she turn to her friend. In the dash lights, Melanie looked as frightened and shaken as Tess felt.

"Melanie, why were you down by the lake? Tell me you didn't come back here to see Royce. He's dangerous!"

Melanie's lips thinned into a grim line as she started the car and pulled onto the road. "I know that. I found that out the hard way, remember?"

"But I'm not sure you realize just how dangerous he is." Haltingly, Tess told her friend about the conversation she'd overheard. When she finished, she was trembling again. "He's going to convince everyone that I stole that bracelet. He's going to make sure I get sent to prison. He said five to ten years—"

"And he would do it, too," Melanie muttered, watching the road almost fiercely. "What if you really are pregnant? What if tries to…to—"

"Kill me?"

Melanie winced. "Surely he wouldn't go that far."

Tess put her hands on her stomach. "I have to see Jared. He'll help me—"

"Are you crazy?" Melanie gave her a quick, frightened glance. "He's not going to take your side in this, Tess. He probably won't even believe you."

"But if I tell him what I heard, he'll have to believe me," she said urgently. The rhythm of the windshield wipers seemed to keep pace with her heartbeat. "How could I have known about the trust if I hadn't overheard Royce talking about it?"

Melanie scowled at the road. "Think about it for a

minute. You said Royce found out through a clerk in his father's attorney's office. If you tell Jared what you know, Royce will just pay that clerk to swear he told you about that trust weeks ago. Royce will make it seem as if you knew about it all along. That's why you went after Jared, because you wanted the money. Think about it, Tess. It all ties together too perfectly. You've never liked the Spencers, and Jared knows that. The two of you have even fought about it. When he starts putting it all together, he'll come to the conclusion Royce wants him to.''

Tess shivered uncontrollably. ''But if I'm pregnant, I have to tell him. I can't keep it from him.''

''You have to! For God's sake, Tess—'' Melanie broke off, glancing in her rearview mirror.

''What's the matter?'' Tess asked anxiously, twisting around in her seat to glance at the road behind them.

A car was coming up behind them, traveling too fast on the wet pavement. The headlights flashed in the rearview mirror, and Melanie squinted at the glare.

Tess swung back around, instinctively gripping the seat. They were approaching a curve, and the car started around them. ''What is he doing?'' Melanie cried. ''He's going to kill us all!''

The road was narrow, and the car, beside them now, began crowding Melanie to the shoulder. As they rounded the curve, the car bumped against them, and Melanie lost control of the wheel. Both she and Tess screamed as the car flew off the road and careened down a steep embankment.

For what seemed like an eternity, the car plunged down the hillside at a dizzying speed, bouncing over rocks and tree stumps, veering wildly first one way, then the other.

A tree loomed before them, and Tess threw up her arm to shield her face. The car smashed against the trunk, and flipped. When all had quieted, Tess found herself upside down and disoriented, certain that she'd suffered some horrible injury. But strangely enough, she felt no pain. She glanced over at Melanie, and her heart almost stopped. The driver's side had taken the brunt of the crash. Melanie was trapped in a mass of twisted metal.

"Melanie! Oh, God," Tess whispered, struggling with her seat belt. She managed to climb out the shattered window, and she staggered around the car.

Falling to her knees, she tried to find a way to free her friend, but the door was smashed inward so badly, Tess couldn't budge it. "Melanie? Please, please be alive!"

Miraculously, Melanie's eyes fluttered open. Blood trickled from the corner of her mouth as she stared up at Tess.

"Did you see the car?" she said on a gasping breath. "It was Royce."

Tess was so horrified and so frightened, she didn't know what to say. "Hang on, Melanie. I'm going for help."

"No! Don't leave me!" she begged. "What if he comes back?"

"I have to call an ambulance—"

"Promise me." Melanie's blue eyes pleaded with Tess. She looked so fragile and so tragic lying in the mangled wreckage.

Tess swallowed her tears. "Anything."

"Whatever happens, don't let Royce find out about the baby."

Chapter Five

"Tess?" Her skin was like ice beneath his hands. Jared felt her tremble, and for one wild moment, he thought about dragging her into his arms, holding her so close she would never be able to leave him again.

But, of course, he couldn't do that. He *wouldn't* do it. Not after what she'd done.

"Did you hear what I said?" he demanded.

"I—no," Tess stammered.

He placed both hands on her arms. "You don't look well. Do you need some water? Should I call someone?"

"No, I'm fine." She glanced at his hands on her arms. "You can let go of me now. I'm not going to faint or anything."

But Jared held on to her. He stared down at her, searching her distraught features, the shadows in her eyes. "Why did you do it? Why did you take my mother's bracelet. To get back at her? At *me?*"

"You asked me the same question back then," she said angrily, "when you came to see me at the sheriff's station. You kept looking for some noble reason. I told you then why I did it. I did it because I wanted to. It was there and I took it."

He frowned down at her. "I don't believe that. There had to be a reason."

"Even if there was, it wouldn't matter now." She made a helpless motion with her hands. "Six years is a long time. A lot's changed."

"You got married," he said. "You had a baby."

She moistened her lips. "Yes."

"It must have happened very quickly. You said Emily is five years old. What did you do? Go straight from my bed to his?"

She lifted her chin and looked him straight in the eye. "Yes. That's exactly what I did."

That should have been the end of it, but Jared couldn't bring himself to release her. Her haunted eyes tore at his resolve. "I don't believe that. The Tess I knew wouldn't have done that."

"Maybe you didn't know me as well as you thought you did," she challenged.

"I know what we had was special. Incredible." His grasp on her tightened. "Don't you remember?"

"We were kids," she said stubbornly. "Of course it was incredible."

Anger flared inside him. "I'm not just talking about the sex. Although God knows, that was great, too. I'm talking about *us*." He let her go, took a step away from her, then spun back. "Do you know why I wanted to see you down by the lake that night?"

She gave a helpless shrug. "Because you—"

"I wanted to ask you to marry me."

It seemed impossible that her face could go so pale. She looked as if he'd just dealt her some horrible death blow. "I didn't know."

"But you knew how I felt," he said harshly.

"Jared—"

"Jared?"

The voice spoke from the doorway, and both Jared and Tess jumped, then whirled toward the sound.

His mother stood in the doorway, and as she stepped into the office, Jared saw that Royce's wife, Ariel, followed, as usual, behind her.

Neither of them had changed in the years Jared had been away. Cressida was still tall, slender, imperiously graceful, and Ariel was still hardly more than a shadow, a small, colorless woman who seemed content to trail along in the powerful wake of her husband and her mother-in-law. They were both expensively groomed. Cressida wore an elegant blue suit that perfectly matched her eyes. Ariel's outfit was a similar style but in an odd green color that couldn't have been less flattering.

As the two women crossed the room, Cressida's curious gaze rested on Tess. "Hello," she said cordially. "I'm Cressida Spencer, Jared's mother. I don't believe we've met."

She extended a hand to Tess, and for a moment, Tess merely stared at her, as if she wasn't quite sure what to do. She accepted Cressida's handshake, but almost immediately pulled her hand away.

"Actually, Mother, you two have met. This is Tess Campbell. Her name used to be Granger."

Cressida furrowed a delicate eyebrow, then recognition sprang to her blue eyes. Her features instantly hardened. "Joelle's daughter?"

Tess looked as if she would have liked nothing more than to crawl into a hole and never come back out. "How are you, Mrs. Spencer?"

"I'm well, thank you." Cressida's demeanor went almost frigid as she glared at Tess, but years of practice had made her adept at social deportment. "How is your mother, Tess?"

"She's well, thank you."

"I'm not sure you've met my sister-in-law, Ariel," Jared said.

"How do you do?" Ariel murmured shyly. She stuck out her hand, too, but it was she who seemed to withdraw her fingers quickly this time. "I'm looking for Royce," she said to Jared. "Do you have any idea where he might be?"

"You tried his office, I presume?"

Ariel nodded. "Yes, but I'll just go and see if he's back." She tucked a limp strand of brown hair behind one ear. "Will you excuse me?"

"Yes, run along, dear." Cressida shooed her away with a crisp wave of her hand. "I need to have a word with Jared."

"Of course," he said. "I'll just be a moment longer." He turned to Tess, having no idea what he was going to say to her, but she beat him to the punch.

"I have to go. There's a lot to do. Thank you...for your help." She clutched the check in her hand. "It means a lot."

Jared moved toward her, but this time he didn't touch her. He stared down at her instead, as if he could hold her in place with his gaze. "Will you keep me informed? Let me know if there's anything else I can do?"

"You've done more than enough," she said, making no commitments. She glanced past him, her demeanor edgy. "Mrs. Spencer." She let her gaze rest on Jared one last time, nodded slightly, then turned and strode from his office.

Fled, actually, was the word that came to Jared's mind.

He stared after her for the longest moment until his mother said behind him, "What on earth was she doing here, Jared? I hope you battened down all your valuables." When he didn't respond, Cressida remarked scornfully, "Well, I can't say the years have been kind to her. I guess her misdeeds have finally caught up with her. She looks terrible. Not that she ever was what I'd consider beautiful. Mildly attractive at best."

Jared still said nothing. But he couldn't seem to tear his gaze from the door through which Tess had just disappeared.

JARED HAD WANTED to marry her.

The words were like a litany inside Tess's head.

She hurried through the secretary's office, ignoring the startled look from the older woman seated behind a computer terminal. "Miss? May I help you?"

Tess didn't answer, but rushed instead into the hallway. The long corridor was deserted, and she took a moment to catch her breath. Leaning back against the wall, she closed her eyes.

Jared had wanted to marry her.

Tess put a trembling hand to her mouth. Would that have made a difference? If she'd known Jared planned to propose to her that night, would she have stayed and fought the Spencers? Fought Royce?

Probably not, she conceded. If it had only been her life at stake, she might have. She might have mustered the courage to put her faith in Jared. To tell him exactly what his brother was up to and trust that he would be able to protect her and their unborn child.

But once his mother's bracelet had been stolen, Tess

had seen the doubt in his eyes. The suspicion. The sheriff had come to the emergency room after her and Melanie's accident to arrest her. She'd been taken to the station for questioning, and she hadn't seen Jared until much later, when she'd finally been released. He'd confronted her then, demanded the truth from her. He hadn't wanted to believe her capable of such a crime, but when she hadn't denied it, what else could he think?

And even if she'd told him the truth, a part of him would always have wondered.

And if she'd told him about Royce? Would he have had doubts about that as well?

It didn't matter. None of it mattered. After the accident, Tess had known only too well what Royce was capable of. In order to protect herself and her baby, she'd let Jared think the worst of her so that he wouldn't pursue her when she left town. And it had worked. He hadn't followed her. In six years, he'd never once tried to contact her.

The elevator doors slid open, and as she hurried across the hallway, she collided with someone getting off. The check and her purse went flying.

"I'm sorry," she murmured, scrambling to retrieve a tube of lipstick that had rolled from her bag.

"No, it was entirely my fault." The man bent and scooped the check from the floor, along with several items from her purse. When he straightened and turned toward Tess, fear curled in her stomach.

Smiling, Royce Spencer gave her nothing more than a quick, apologetic glance, a casual perusal. "I think that's everything." He held out the items from her purse—car keys, wallet, an ink pen—and Tess reluctantly let him drop them into her purse. With a flourish, he palmed the check, faceup, like a waiter presenting the bill. "Also yours?"

Tess swallowed. "Yes, thank you." With nervous fingers, she plucked the check from his hand, praying that, like Jared, he hadn't recognized her, that he hadn't seen her name on the bank draft or the signature at the bottom.

She moved toward the elevator, but he stepped in front of her, blocking her way. He was bigger than she remembered, even taller than Jared. And he'd put on weight. Gone was the lean, muscular physique that had made him seem dangerously predatory six years ago.

"Just a minute." He'd been holding the elevator open with one hand, but now he let the doors slide closed. "Do I know you?"

Before Tess could answer, recognition flickered in his dark eyes, followed swiftly by suspicion, and then, oddly enough, amusement. "Tess? Tess Granger?"

"It's Tess Campbell now."

"My God," he said. "I almost didn't recognize you." His brown gaze, more intense this time, moved over her, making Tess shiver with dread.

She tried to move around him and press the elevator button, but again he blocked her way.

"Hold on. I can't let you just run off. It's been… how long?" He was elegantly dressed in a gray suit and silk tie, but the years had not been all that kind to him. He was only twenty-eight, two years younger than Jared, but he looked older. The weight gain was most prominent in his face, the fullness and slightly sagging jawline adding at least a decade. He was still a handsome man, more traditionally handsome than Jared perhaps, but the hardness in his eyes, the secret knowledge that Tess possessed, made his features seem almost reptilian.

"How's your mother?" he asked in a smooth, liquid voice. He was playing it light, charming. He had no idea that she knew he'd been the one to set her up. That he'd been willing to take even more drastic measures if she hadn't accepted his father's offer to leave town. But it wasn't just the threat of prison that had driven Tess from Eden. That had made her refuse Jared's offer of help. It was the accident that had put Melanie in a wheelchair for the rest of her life.

"We missed her out at the lake house after she resigned," Royce was saying. "Of course, it was impossible for her to stay on after…that unfortunate incident." His smiled turned contemplative. "You know, Tess, I never did get a chance to talk to you after that night, but I always wanted you to know that I understood why you did it. It would have been tempting for anyone in your position."

White-hot anger rolled over Tess, and she had to turn away quickly before he saw the rage in her eyes.

"I was always glad that the family didn't press charges. After you agreed to leave town to avoid any…unpleasantness, there didn't seem to be a reason to."

"Yes," Tess said, turning to face him. "I didn't want there to be any unpleasantness."

If he noticed the bitterness in her voice, he decided to ignore it. "At any rate, we sold the lake house not long after that. Without Joelle around to take care of things, the place started falling apart. But you know what they say, good help is hard to find."

"Yes, that's what they say. If you'll excuse me—" Tess tried once again to move around him, but he wasn't ready to let her go. Like a cat toying with a mouse, he hadn't yet had his fun.

"So what brings you here?" His voice remained friendly and he kept right on smiling, but Tess wasn't fooled.

She slipped the check into her purse, buying herself some time until a suitable excuse popped into her head. "Actually, it's funny that you should mention the lake house because that's exactly why I'm here. I'm living back in Eden now, and I own a cleaning service." She extracted a card from her purse and handed it to him. "I wondered if your family had anyone looking after the house. Of course, I didn't realize you'd sold it."

"Your mother didn't tell you?" The amusement was back in his eyes as he gazed down at the card. "Eden's Maid Brigade. Catchy." He glanced up. "Even if we still owned the place, you might be a hard sale to my mother, everything considered."

Tess thought about the coldness in Cressida Spencer's eyes, and she had to suppress a shudder. "Yes," she said, clearing her throat. "You're probably right about that. But I didn't think there was any harm in asking."

He shook his head. "A maid service, huh? Like mother, like daughter."

It's good, honest work, Tess wanted to tell him, but now was not the time to get into a discussion of morals. Certainly not with Royce Spencer. She shrugged. "It's a living."

"Well, I'm afraid I can't help you out. We don't own any property in Eden anymore."

"I understand." She forced a smile, but her muscles felt rigid, unnatural. "Well, I won't keep you..."

The elevator doors finally opened again, and a man

got out. He said something to Royce, and while Royce's attention was diverted, Tess darted inside the car. But Royce's right arm shot out to retract the doors.

He turned quickly, stepping into the car with Tess. "I'll ride down a couple of floors with you."

As the doors slid together, Tess saw Ariel Spencer come hurrying toward the elevators, her pale face taut, her demeanor agitated. Whether she meant to call out or not, Tess never knew because the doors closed in Ariel's face.

Trapped in an elevator with Royce Spencer was a nightmare come true for Tess. She felt almost sick as the car began to descend.

She stared straight ahead, not even glancing at his reflection in the mirrored walls, but she could feel his gaze on her. The hair at the back of her neck rose in fear.

"What have you been doing to yourself, Tess?" he asked softly. "You don't look well."

The quality of his voice, that barest hint of danger, made panic bubble inside her. She kept her gaze on the wall in front of her. "Thanks for your concern, but I'm fine."

"I hope so." He reached across her and pushed the button for a lower floor. His arm grazed hers, and it was all Tess could do not to flinch. "Well," he said, "it's really been great seeing you. Give my regards to your mother. And to that friend of yours. What was her name? Melanie? A great-looking girl. Damn shame what happened to her that night. You were a lot more fortunate."

Tess's heart began to beat in slow, painful strokes as memories assaulted her. Memories of the terror in Melanie's eyes, the bruises on her arms. *"Royce said*

*if I told anyone, he'd kill me. And I believe him. You
don't know how dangerous he is—"*

*"Well, in that case, I'd just have to find a more per-
manent solution, wouldn't I? One that would get rid of
the kid, too."*

Royce cocked his head as he gazed down at Tess
now. "Are you sure you're okay? You look a little
pale."

"I'm fine," Tess managed to answer. She caught a
glimpse of her reflection in one of the mirrors. Her eyes
were wide, haunted, a little too bright, and there was
fear in her expression, in the way she held herself
stiffly, in the way her features seemed frozen in place.
It took every ounce of her strength to subdue the terror.

The car stopped, and as the doors opened Royce
said, "You be sure and tell Melanie that Royce Spencer says hello, hear? Tell her I haven't forgotten her."

He got out, and the doors slowly began to close between them. But at the last minute, he stopped them
again. "Oh, and Tess? I almost forgot. I hope you find
your little girl."

"YOU NEVER ANSWERED my question," Cressida said
coolly. "What was Tess Granger doing in your office?
I'm surprised she didn't end up in prison after she left
Eden."

Jared whirled, suddenly furious with his mother's
needling. "All that business happened six years ago,"
he snapped. "You don't know the kind of person Tess
is today any more than I do."

Cressida gave him a piercing look. "A leopard can't
change its spots, as they say."

"That may be true," Jared agreed. "But I've never
been completely convinced that Tess was guilty."

His mother stared at him as if he'd lost his mind. "For God's sake, Jared, my bracelet was found in her purse. A witness saw her put it there. And on top of that, she left town after your father agreed not to press charges. What more proof do you need?"

She was right, Jared thought. The evidence against Tess had been overwhelming, not the least of which was her own admission of guilt. But even then, he hadn't been able to believe it. To accept it. He couldn't have been that wrong about her.

But apparently he had been.

Jared moved to the window and glanced out. Nine stories below, a woman hurried across the street, so preoccupied she glanced neither left nor right for on-coming traffic. Horn blaring, a car screeched to a halt only a few inches from her. The woman threw up her hands defensively, and as she spun toward the car, Jared caught a brief glance of her face. It was Tess.

His heart jumped at the close call, and he uncon-sciously put out a hand toward the window, as if to help her.

Why was she so hell-bent on getting away that she'd almost gotten herself run over? Was her agitation be-cause of her daughter? Or could it be that whatever she'd been running from six years ago was still driving her away?

For years, Jared had fantasized about seeing Tess again, letting her know exactly what he thought of her. But the moment he'd recognized her, the moment he'd glimpsed the pain in her eyes and the despair in her face, the last six years simply disappeared. His anger and bitterness at her betrayal seemed trivial in com-parison to a missing child.

He frowned at the street scene below. The driver had

gotten out of the car, and by the looks of his expression, was berating Tess for her carelessness. And she was apologizing, hands out appealingly. The driver would have to be hard-hearted, indeed, not to respond, because in spite of her haggard appearance, there was still something very appealing about Tess.

It was hard to imagine her married to anyone else after what they'd shared that summer. Hard to imagine she had a daughter with another man, but then, maybe it was as she'd said—she and Jared were never meant to be together.

Is that why she'd stolen the bracelet? he wondered. To prove how wrong they were for each other?

He watched her disappear into the parking garage below as a thousand memories crashed over him. Tess, in the pool that day. Tess, lying beside him on his boat, watching the stars. Tess, in his arms. Tess, gazing up at him defiantly. *"I wanted it, okay? I saw it lying there, so I took it. Now, do you still want me?"*

And God help him, he had.

"I hope you're not thinking of taking back up with her," Cressida said.

Jared shrugged. "If I am, it is my business."

Cressida sighed. "Must I remind you that you are operating at the mercy of a very conservative board, Jared? They've expressed concern about your age and lack of experience. A liaison with the wrong sort of person would only reinforce their trepidation. On the other hand, the right sort of union would go a long way in calming troubled waters."

"And you have someone in mind, no doubt," Jared said in an irritated tone.

Cressida smoothed back her white-blond hair. "You and Lauren Mathison make a lovely couple. She's beautiful and charming, and she comes from the right sort of people. You and she share so much in common. You went to the same schools, you move in the same circles. She could be a real asset to you with the board.''

''Let's get one thing straight, shall we?'' Jared walked over and stood behind his desk. ''My personal life is off-limits to the board. And to you.''

Cressida gave him a cool assessment. ''I'm simply looking out for your best interests, Jared. I know how important it is to you to follow in your father's footsteps.''

''Actually,'' Jared said slowly, ''I'm beginning to think it was always a lot more important to him than it was to me. I was happy managing the New Orleans Spencer.''

''Yes, but you have to think of the good of the company. You're needed here now. And like it or not, this position comes with certain obligations. Certain expectations.''

''Like hooking up with the right sort of woman,'' he said dryly.

Cressida ignored his sarcasm. ''Exactly.''

''Well, I'm sorry to disappoint you, Mother, but I have no intention of marrying Lauren Mathison. I'm not in love with her, and she knows it.''

Cressida's finely tweezed eyebrows lifted. ''Who said anything about love? The best marriages are made with far more consideration than mere love.''

Yes, Jared thought. *Like the loveless pairing you shared with my father.* Still, he supposed she had a point. He'd been in love with Tess Granger, and look how that had turned out. Aloud, he said accusingly, ''You know, Mother, just because someone had the presumption to plant an item in the newspaper calling Lauren my fiancée doesn't make it so. In fact, I don't think I'll be seeing much of her from now on.''

''Why on earth not? She's perfect for you, Jared.''

''That's not for you to decide.''

Cressida's lips thinned in disapproval. ''Well, I certainly hope your decision has nothing to do with Tess Granger.''

''And if it does?''

''I won't stand for it,'' she said coldly. ''I simply won't stand for it. I will not allow that woman to worm her way into this family. I won't allow her to tarnish our good name.''

''What have you always had against her?'' Jared demanded.

''You can ask that, after what she did?''

Jared shook his head. ''You didn't like her before that. And she knew it. That's why she wanted to keep our relationship a secret that summer. She knew you'd give her a hard time. You know, Mother, if I didn't know better, I'd say you felt threatened by Tess. Maybe you still do.''

''Threatened?'' Cressida's chin lifted in outrage. ''Don't be ridiculous!''

''Maybe the reason you never liked her,'' Jared challenged, ''was because she had the audacity to consider herself an equal to the Spencers.''

''So there *is* something going on between the two of you.'' Cressida's voice had gone almost calm. Too calm.

''Not that I feel the need to explain, but Tess's visit wasn't personal.'' He held up the newspaper turned to Emily's picture. ''Have you heard about this?''

Cressida took the paper from him and glanced at the

headline. "That missing little girl? Yes, of course, it's been all over the news for the past several days. What does that have to do with Tess Granger?"

"This is her daughter," Jared said grimly. "She disappeared from a school playground almost three weeks ago."

A gasp sounded from across the room, and Jared looked up to see Ariel standing just inside the doorway, her hand at her heart. "Oh, no," she said in a near whisper. "Oh, dear God, no."

Chapter Six

Standing at her kitchen window the next morning, Tess watched the bleak, shadowy hues of daybreak slowly melt away as the sun topped the horizon. She'd always liked early morning, the hour or so she had to herself before Emily awakened and the day began in earnest— the rushed breakfasts and hurried goodbye kisses, the mad dashes to school, the million and one tiny details that were a part of every single mother's routine. How Tess longed for that harried sameness now.

She wrapped her arms around her middle, trying to beat back the feeling of isolation, the killing loneliness that tightened like a vise around her heart. *I can't do this,* she thought helplessly. *I can't do this alone.*

She wasn't alone, of course. She had her mother and Melanie, other friends and neighbors who had given her their unfailing support. But it wasn't the same as having someone by her side, going through everything she was going through, experiencing the grief and the terror and knowing without having to ask why she couldn't eat, why, even in exhaustion, she fought sleep because of the nightmares.

She thought of Jared, briefly, then tried to turn her mind away. But it wasn't that easy. His image had hovered at the fringes of her consciousness ever since she'd seen him yesterday, but it was Royce's face she saw when she closed her eyes. Royce's parting words that had tormented her all through the sleepless night.

"Oh, and Tess? I hope you find your little girl."

It wasn't unusual that Royce would know about the kidnapping. Emily's disappearance had been thoroughly publicized, not just locally but all over the state. Her picture was in all the papers, and Tess had appeared on TV.

But that rationalization didn't stop her blood from going cold when she thought about the way he'd stared down at her. The look in his eyes…

Clenching her fists, Tess summoned her strength, called on every ounce of courage she possessed not to give in to the panic, to the almost overwhelming urge to confide in someone, to share her burden.

But not just with anyone. With Jared. Six years ago she'd made a deal with his father to leave town in order to avoid having charges brought against her for the stolen bracelet, in order to avoid going to prison. She'd allowed Jared to believe her guilty of the crime so that he would let her go.

But it was the accident that had really driven her away. As she'd gazed down into Melanie's blood-streaked face, the full impact of what she was up against had hit Tess. She had known then just how far Royce Spencer was willing to go to win. And it wasn't just Tess who stood in his way. It was her child.

"Emily," she whispered, putting her fingertips on the cool glass pane. "Where are you, baby? Where *are* you?"

THIRTY MINUTES LATER, Tess pulled up outside the volunteer center, which had been set up in a community faciiity in downtown Eden a few blocks over from the Jefferson County Sheriff's Office.

For days following Emily's disappearance, the center had been a beehive of activity, with hundreds of volunteers pouring in to help in the search-and-rescue efforts. They came from cities, they came from towns, they came from remote rural areas in the far corners of the state. They came from different backgrounds, with different insights and motivations, but they came, nonetheless. College students passed out flyers alongside seasoned off-duty policemen. Construction workers beat the bushes with agents from the FBI, the Mississippi Highway Patrol and the Jefferson County Sheriff's Office. They were different, yes, but they all came with the same goal: to find Emily and bring her home safely.

But now, after nearly three weeks, most of the volunteers had gone home, and the remaining personnel seemed utterly dejected. To a person, they could hardly look Tess in the eye as she walked into the building that Saturday morning.

It wasn't their fault, of course. They'd done everything humanly possibly to find her little girl, and Tess would be forever grateful to them for their tireless devotion and sacrifice. But now they were going home, returning to their normal lives, and it was left up to her to carry on the search. To make sure her daughter didn't become another tragic statistic.

Across the room, some of the computers stations were being dismantled and the equipment packed in boxes to be transported back to the local businesses that had loaned them to the cause. Tess blinked back tears as she turned away.

But all hope wasn't yet lost. There were still a dozen or so volunteers who showed up faithfully every day, and now they had a new cause, a renewed fervor. The updated reward information had been printed on flyers late yesterday afternoon, and they would all work feverishly for the next several hours, addressing and stamping envelopes, sorting and bagging the mail for the post office to deliver all over the country, where the flyers would be distributed by other volunteers, missing-persons organizations and law enforcement personnel.

"How are you feeling this morning?" Melanie asked when Tess sat down beside her.

Tess shrugged. "Like I've felt every morning since she's been gone." She dragged a hand through her hair. "Empty. Dead inside. Like my heart has been ripped out of me. Sometimes when I wake up in the middle of the night, it seems like all this is just a bad dream. That if I go down the hallway, I'll find her in her bed, curled up with her teddy bear, sleeping soundly. Then I remember. Then it all comes rushing back to me, and I just don't know how I'm going to get through the rest of the night. Or the next day. Or the rest of my life."

Melanie reached over and took her hand. "It's going to be okay. You're not alone in this, Tess."

"I know."

"The volunteer center may be officially shutting down, but I'm not going anywhere, and neither are they." Melanie waved her hand toward the busy group of women huddled over the folding tables. "We're going to be right here every spare moment, doing what we've been doing for the last two and a half weeks. And if not here, then somewhere else. We'll find a new place and start up our own volunteer center. Maybe we can use one of the smaller meeting rooms here. I'll talk to the other town council members about it.'' Melanie had been elected to the town council a year ago, and was very active in her civic duties.

Tess forced a smile. "I don't know what I'd do without you."

It was true. Melanie had spent hours on top of hours at the center since Emily's disappearance. Together, she and Naomi Cross had worked diligently to set up a nationwide poster-distribution program and a telephone and computer networking system that coordinated local efforts with national organizations that dealt with missing children. She'd also tirelessly manned phone banks and stuffed envelopes, like everyone else, and all that after she'd completed her workday at Fairhaven Academy. But her most valuable contribution had been her moral support.

"I'll never be able to thank you enough," Tess said. "Any of you."

"Nobody here wants any thanks. All we want is to find Emily."

Tess's throat clogged. "I know that."

"Tess—" Melanie leaned forward, lowering her voice. "What happened yesterday with Jared? I know you got the money, but you didn't tell him about—"

"Emily?" Tess shook her head. "No, I didn't tell him. I didn't have to. Once he learned she was missing, he just sat down and wrote me out a check. No questions asked."

Something flickered in Melanie's eyes. "As easy as that?"

No, Tess thought. It hadn't been easy. Nothing about her visit to Jared had been easy, but seeing Royce again, having him inquire first about Melanie and then mentioning Emily's disappearance…

Melanie touched her arm. "Are you okay?"

Tess glanced at her friend. "I think there's something I should tell you," she said worriedly.

Melanie seemed to brace herself. Her fingers tightened around the arms of her wheelchair. "What is it?"

"I saw Royce yesterday."

The color drained from Melanie's face. "Where?"

"He was just getting off the elevator as I was getting on. I bumped into him. He didn't recognize me at first, but then…"

Melanie stared at her in dread. "What happened? What did he do?"

Again Tess hesitated, not certain she was doing the right thing by telling Melanie about her confrontation with Royce. But at the same time, she didn't think she should keep it from her, either. "He asked about you."

Melanie's knuckles whitened on the arms of her chair.

"He talked about the accident," Tess said. "And then he told me to tell you that he hasn't forgotten you."

"Oh, God—"

"Melanie, it's okay." Tess put her hand over Melanie's. "He can't hurt you now. I won't let him."

"How can you stop him?" Melanie wrested her hand from Tess's grasp. "I knew this would happen. Why? *Why* did you have to go there?"

Tess drew back in the face of her friend's anguish. "You know why I went. I had to."

"No, you didn't. We could have figured out a way to get the money. There's no guarantee offering a reward will help anyway. And now that Jared knows about Emily... God, Tess. Don't you see what you've done?''

"Melanie—"

"You've brought them back into our lives. We're all in danger now."

"Melanie, please," Tess said, glancing around the command center. She lowered her voice. "Think about it. There's no reason for Royce to come after you now. He has a family. He has the trust. That's all he ever wanted."

Melanie gave her a bitter look. "I'm all too aware of that."

"He doesn't know about Emily. He can't."

"And what about Jared?"

Tess's heart tightened at the thought of him, but she hardened her resolve. "He isn't a threat. There's no reason why he should suspect anything. He's been out of my life for a long time."

"If he's out of your life," Melanie said harshly, "then what's he doing here?"

TESS SPUN, and from across the room, her gaze collided with Jared's. The impact was almost a physical jolt. Every muscle in Jared's body tightened as he became overly aware of the attraction. It was still there. Undeniably. God help him, Tess still had the same effect on him. The same hold over him.

Today she wore jeans and a simple cotton blouse that made her appear even thinner. Her hair was pulled back into a ponytail, and Jared saw that it still hung in spirals, although the golden highlights were gone, along with the luster. Her tragedy had taken a toll.

As he moved across the room toward her, her face mirrored some of the emotions he felt at that moment—

confusion, anger, trepidation. And, yes, even the attraction, although he didn't think she'd admit to that.

"What are you doing here?" she asked with a frown when he stopped before her.

"I came to see if there was anything else I could do to help."

A look of alarm flashed across her face. "But... you've already done so much."

"Surely no effort is enough until your daughter is brought home safe and sound."

Tess looked as if she didn't quite know what to do or say to that, and Jared could sympathize. In truth, he was a little puzzled by his actions, as well. He wasn't sure why he'd come here except that he'd lain awake all last night, thinking about Tess and worrying about her daughter. He couldn't get either one of them out of his mind. And then come morning, the need to drive up to Eden, to see Tess again, to find out if there'd been any news had been overwhelming.

So he'd skipped out on a Saturday-morning board meeting, although he knew that would garner a black mark against him. He'd canceled lunch with Lauren, racquetball with his brother, and here he was.

Suddenly uncomfortable, he glanced around the community center. His arrival had generated momentary interest, but everyone except for Tess and the woman beside her had gone back to work. Folding tables and chairs, littered with stacks of flyers, envelopes, staplers, rubber bands and various other office paraphernalia, were scattered about the large room, and the walls and windows were papered with Emily's picture. Everywhere Jared turned, her dark eyes stared down at him. And below her picture the terrible question: Have you seen this child?

My God, he thought. How did Tess stand it?

"How did you know where to find me?" she asked, meeting his gaze head-on. She'd lifted her chin slightly, but there was an unmistakable edge to her voice, an indefinable flicker in her eyes that might have been fear.

Jared shrugged. "I went by the sheriff's station and spoke to a detective named Cross."

"Abby?"

"That's her. She told me you'd probably be here." He glanced around the room again. Despite the activity, the place seemed empty, subdued. Sergeant Cross had warned him that the volunteer center was being shut down, although the investigation would remain active.

"It had better," Jared had told her gravely. "Because if I have to, I'll get the governor involved in this case."

"Really?" Sergeant Cross had given him one of those cool, assessing glances that cops seemed to master so easily. "And just what is your interest in this case, Mr. Spencer?"

"I'm a friend of the little girl's mother."

No comment at that, but a slightly raised eyebrow had warned Jared that Sergeant Cross wouldn't take kindly to outside interference.

His gaze came back to settle on Tess. "Have you been here every day since your daughter disappeared?"

"No, not at first. The police wanted me to stay home by the phone, even though they'd put a tap on the line and a deputy was there twenty-four hours a day to monitor the calls. But I almost went crazy waiting for the phone to ring, praying that the next call would be news of Emily, and praying that it wouldn't be. So I started coming down here where I felt I could be more useful.''

Jared glanced up at one of the posters on the wall. Again he experienced an inexplicable sorrow, a deep gnawing worry for the little girl's safety. ''Could we go somewhere and talk?''

Tess looked startled. ''No, I don't think so. There's a lot to do here—''

''It won't take long.''

She glanced down at the young woman in the wheelchair beside her. Jared had noticed her when he'd first walked in, but Tess had made no move to introduce them. He'd assumed she was a volunteer and that perhaps Tess didn't know her all that well, but now, as the young woman glanced up at him, Jared was struck by the coolness in her blue eyes, the bitter curl of her full lips.

She was very beautiful, her features almost angelic on first glance. But beneath the perfect facade, a hardness lurked. Something Jared couldn't quite define glinted in her eyes.

He happened to be looking at her when Tess murmured, ''I'll be right back, Melanie.''

The hostility that flashed across the woman's face was almost breathtaking, but she schooled her emotions before glancing up at Tess.

''Are you sure you want to do this?'' she asked softly.

Tess put a hand on the woman's shoulder, as if to reassure her. Then she turned to Jared and nodded toward the far side of the room. ''There're some offices just down that hallway. We can probably find an empty one.''

She led the way, and as they crossed the community

center, Jared's gaze lifted to a faded banner across the stage. Eden, Mississippi. Where Heaven Meets Earth.

A chill shot through him even though the air was quite warm inside the hall.

TESS WALKED straight over to the window and stared out.

There was a park across the street, but it was too early for children to be out and about. Later, a few would come to play, but not alone. Never alone since Emily's disappearance. The older ones would come in groups, the younger ones accompanied by their parents. They would swing and slide and climb on the jungle gyms while the mothers huddled together on the benches, talking in low tones, wondering aloud how something like this could happen in their town. And all the while, thankful, so terribly grateful, that it hadn't happened to their child.

"Who is the young woman in the wheelchair?" Jared asked behind her.

Her attention was so focused on the playground that for a moment Tess thought he was referring to someone in the park. She turned to face him. "Excuse me?"

He nodded toward the door. "The woman in the wheelchair. You called her Melanie. She looks familiar."

"You don't remember her?" Tess asked in surprise. "I guess you never met her, but she was driving the car the night I was in that accident. The same night I was arrested."

He frowned. "I was told the accident wasn't serious. You walked away with barely a scratch."

And Melanie hadn't walked away at all, Tess thought with a pang of guilt. "I was led away from the emergency room in handcuffs, to be exact," she said with an edge of defiance.

Jared winced. "I didn't know about that, either. I looked everywhere for you that night."

"When all along, there I was, sitting in jail."

"You sound as if you're proud of that accomplishment," he said accusingly.

Tess lifted her chin. "I'm not proud of a lot of things that happened back then, but they did happen. And they are in the past. I don't see any point in looking back."

His gaze on her deepened. "It was always easy for you, wasn't it? Everything was always black and white."

"Easy for me?" She gave a caustic laugh. "That's good, coming from you. The fortunate son."

"It always comes back to that, doesn't it? You were always such a snob, Tess."

She sputtered in astonishment. "A...snob? That's ridiculous."

"Is it?" One eyebrow lifted. "You think only people with money can be snobs? You never tried to hide your disdain for the north side of the lake. For people anywhere who had wealth. But especially for my family. You wore your working-class background like a badge of pride, and I used to wonder sometimes if that's what drove us apart. If that's why you really left that summer."

"You know why I left." Tess strove to keep the bitterness from her voice. "It was either leave town or go to jail."

"I never would have let that happen, and you know it."

"There might not have been anything you could have done to stop it."

His gaze on her narrowed. "You never did give me much credit, did you?"

"On the contrary," she said coolly. "I always gave your entire family a great deal of credit."

"Hard to believe," he said grimly. "Six years later, and nothing has changed between us."

She shrugged helplessly. "So why are you here?"

"At the moment, I'm damned if I know." His gaze searched her face, as if he expected to find the answer in her expression. He turned away in frustration, rubbing the back of his neck. "Ever since I saw you yesterday, I've been asking myself why you *did* take that bracelet. It wasn't for its value. You scorned money."

"Maybe I came to realize exactly what it is that money can buy." This time, Tess made no effort to hide her bitterness.

"Meaning?

Because with enough money, you can buy your way out of anything, she wanted to tell him. Even attempted murder. Turning back to the window, she said instead, "You didn't drive all the way up here just to rehash the past."

"That's not the only reason I came, no," he agreed. "But I do want some answers. You owe me that much."

Her mouth tightened in anger. "I should have known there would be strings attached to Spencer money."

"Why is it," he asked with his own anger, "that you always have to make me the enemy?"

"I don't. I didn't—"

"Yes, you did. You never could forgive yourself for falling in love with me, could you?"

Tess opened her mouth to protest, but instead she bit back her retort because his words held an inkling of truth. Back then, Jared had represented the very things she'd grown up despising—wealth, power, social status. She'd always resented that her mother had to work for his family, and a part of Tess had felt that, in loving Jared, she was betraying who she was and where she'd come from, that she was diminishing her own self-worth somehow.

She'd been a lot more insecure than she'd ever realized, Tess thought. And maybe Jared was right. Maybe her uncertainty in herself had driven her away from him as much as her fear had.

Staring at him now, she saw the changes the years had wrought. He was still a young man, only thirty, but there was a new maturity in his features, a sureness in his demeanor. There was also a hardness in his eyes, a cynical twist to his mouth that bespoke his rapid climb up the corporate ladder—and what he'd done to get there. He'd grown more confident over the years, more devastatingly handsome, while Tess—

She drew a long breath. She didn't want to think how she must look to him.

He moved across the room toward her, making her stomach tighten in apprehension.

"Why did you leave that summer, Tess? It wasn't just about the bracelet. You had to have known I wouldn't let you go to prison. I've always believed there was more to it than that."

She rubbed a hand across her face. "Why do you even care. You're engaged, for God's sake."

He stared at her blankly for a moment. "Engaged?"

Too late Tess realized her mistake. If she told him about seeing the picture of him and his fiancée in the paper, he might read too much into it. He might think she'd being keeping track of him, and she didn't want that. She didn't want him to know that even after six years, the sight of him with a beautiful woman had made her stomach churn sickeningly.

She tried to shrug off her remark. "I just don't understand why it still matters to you, that's all."

"Call me crazy," he said with an edge of sarcasm, "but I've never understood why you didn't trust me enough to tell me the truth. We were in love, for God's sake."

The nerves in her stomach clamped even tighter, but Tess struggled to keep her emotions from showing. "If you really loved me, you would have come after me."

"What?"

"After I left town, you never tried to find me, did you?"

"You said you didn't want to see me anymore—"

"And you believed that, just like you believed I stole your mother's bracelet."

He gazed at her incredulously. "You told me you took the bracelet. You told me you didn't want to see me anymore. What was I supposed to do?"

Tess shrugged. "I'm just saying if you loved me as much as you say you did, if you'd really wanted to marry me, you would have come after me, no matter what."

Digging his fingers through his hair, he swore violently. "You always did make up your own rules, damn it. You were always putting me to some kind of test that I invariably failed, no matter what. I never could figure you out. I still can't."

"Then don't try."

"God, you've got a nerve." The depth of his anger almost took her breath away. "I got over you a long time ago. I hadn't even thought of you in years, and then, out of the blue, you showed up in my office yesterday. You came to me, and I'll gladly do whatever I can to help you find your daughter. But it doesn't come without a price.''

Tess turned back to the window, feeling weak and shaky all over. She was running on nothing but sheer willpower these days. She could muster whatever strength necessary to search for Emily, but she couldn't deal with Jared. She couldn't confront their past. Not now.

''What do you want from me, Jared?''

He put his hands on her arms and turned her to face him. ''Just answers. Just the truth.''

Her eyes squeezed closed. ''Please. I can't do this right now. I can't think of anything but my daughter.''

''Tess—''

''What are you doing to her? Let her go!''

The frightened voice from the doorway caused them both to start. Jared glanced over his shoulder to where Melanie sat framed in the doorway, but he didn't release Tess. If anything, his grasp on her arms tightened possessively.

Melanie rolled into the room, her blue gaze trained on Jared. There was fear in her gaze, but also defiance. Also hatred. ''Who do you think you are, bullying her at a time like this? You ought to be ashamed of yourself.''

Jared frowned as he stared down at Tess. ''I wasn't trying to bully you—''

''That's exactly what you were doing,'' Melanie retorted before Tess could say anything. ''You may be a Spencer, but that doesn't mean you can't observe common decency. Can't you see she's ready to collapse? My God, look at her. She hasn't eaten anything in days, and I doubt she's slept. She's got enough on her mind without having to deal with you.''

"It's okay, Melanie," Tess murmured.

"No, it's not," she retorted.

Jared dropped his hands from Tess's arms. He took a step back from her, his features going almost rigid. "She's right. This isn't the time or place. I didn't come here to make things worse for you..." He trailed off as his gaze on her darkened. "I'm sorry. In light of what you're going through, I understand how the past would seem trivial to you."

Something in his gaze, in his tone, made Tess's heart start to pound in earnest. Trivial? There was nothing about the past or her feelings for Jared that were trivial. Complicated. Dangerous. But not trivial.

He suddenly looked very remote, very formal, very Spencerish, as if the intimate discussion of the last few minutes had never taken place. "I'll go now. But if there's anything I can do to help, please call me. I mean that."

Tess nodded, unable to speak.

Jared strode past Melanie to the door, then turned, his gaze meeting Tess's for one brief second. "And just for the record? I'm not engaged."

Chapter Seven

"Tess! Tess! Wait a second!" Willa Banks, a volunteer at the center, came puffing across the parking lot toward Tess late that evening as she stowed boxes of flyers and envelopes in the back of her Explorer.

Tess closed the door, and as she waited for the older woman to catch up with her, she turned toward the street, her attention caught by a faded red compact that drove by. Was it her imagination, or had the car slowed as it passed the community center? Had she seen that vehicle somewhere else?

Before Emily's disappearance, a passing car wouldn't have garnered a second look, a moment's thought, but now even the ordinary seemed suspicious to Tess. Every strange vehicle might hold a secret. Every unknown driver might be the one who had lured Emily from the playground.

Shivering, Tess watched the car disappear around the corner before she turned away.

Willa Banks placed a hand over her heart, trying to catch her breath as she hurried up to Tess's truck. Her plump cheeks were bright red from her effort, and her short, gray hair coiled about her face in the heat. Twilight had fallen, but the temperature still hovered in the nineties. The hint of fall Tess imagined yesterday had disappeared with a new front that had dropped just enough rain last night to stir a sweltering humidity.

Willa fanned her face with one hand as she thrust a white box toward Tess. "I made some cookies this morning, but I didn't have enough to pass out to the volunteers so I saved them for you." When Tess hesitated, she said enticingly, "Oatmeal raisin. They're your favorite, aren't they?"

They were Emily's favorite, too.

Tess took the box and tried to thank the older woman, but she waved off Tess's gratitude. "Oh, you know I'm happy to do what I can. After all, Emily is one of our own." Willa was the nurse at Fairhaven Academy. Like many of the staff from Emily's school, she'd become a regular fixture at the volunteer center. Wearing her trademark happy-face pin, she dropped by almost every afternoon and on Saturdays to dole out homemade cookies and doughnuts with the same efficient good humor with which she dispensed sugar-free lollipops and stickers to ailing students.

"I'm sorry I couldn't get to the center earlier today," she said. "But I'm helping put together a safety program to present to the kindergartners and first-graders at Fairhaven on Monday. I spent most of the morning at the sheriff's station." Her eyes gleamed with excitement. "My father was a policeman, you know, so I'm quite comfortable working with the deputy in charge of the program. I've always been fascinated with law enforcement."

"Sounds like a worthwhile program," Tess murmured, eager to be off. She was on her way over to her mother's for dinner, and then the two of them planned to spend the rest of the evening stuffing envelopes. Tess fervently hoped that Melanie hadn't said anything to Joelle about Jared's visit to the volunteer center earlier that morning, although knowing Melanie, she might have. She'd been very upset, so much so that she'd avoided Tess for the rest of the day.

Tess hated to think of her friend at home, alone and frightened, but she wasn't up to going over there tonight to make amends. She didn't want to have to justify her actions yet again to Melanie. Tess had gone to see Jared yesterday because she'd had no other choice. It was as simple as that.

And the reason he'd showed up at the volunteer center this morning? Tess didn't even want to contemplate his motivation.

"It's so important that we teach the children how to protect themselves from strangers, but at the same time find a way to empower them," Willa was saying. "But it's so difficult because Emily's kidnapping has just terrified them—" She broke off, catching herself.

"It's okay," Tess said. "I understand why the children are afraid. Everyone is." It was the same all over town. Parents didn't want to let their children out of sight, and even adults who were caught out alone after dark found themselves glancing over their shoulders, jumping at shadows. No one felt safe. In a place that had been named for paradise, evil had come to call.

"Well," Willa said, patting Tess's arm, "I just wanted you to know why I wasn't here earlier."

"You don't have to explain. I appreciate everything you've done."

Willa said worriedly, "What are you going to do now that the volunteer center is closing?"

"Actually, we may be able to stay on here at the community center. Melanie is going to petition the town council for permission to use one of the smaller meeting rooms.''

"Why Melanie?"

"She's a member of the council."

"Oh, I forgot about that." Willa looked a little uneasy as she peered up at Tess. "I know this is none of my business, Tess, and you can tell me to butt out if you've a mind to. But I couldn't help noticing when I came into the center this afternoon that there seemed to be some tension between you and Melanie. Is everything okay?"

"Everything's fine," Tess said, surprised by the older woman's perception.

Willa's lips pursed almost imperceptibly. "I just mentioned it because I know Melanie has a tendency to be a little high-strung, and the last thing you need is more pressure right now."

A note of disapproval in her voice, made Tess bristle slightly. "Melanie's been a good friend to me, Miss Willa. I would be the last person to criticize her for anything, especially considering all she's been through."

"Oh, I know. I don't mean to suggest…" Willa trailed off, her expression contrite. "I'm sorry. The two of you have been friends for a long time, haven't you?"

"Since we were kids."

"It's only natural that you would defend her, especially considering that…well, you were in the car with her when she had the accident, weren't you?" Before Tess could say anything, Willa murmured, "I suppose her resentment is only natural."

"Resentment?" Tess asked in astonishment. "What are you talking about?"

"You can't see it, can you?" Again, that inflection in her voice. The barest hint of something unpleasant.

What did Willa Banks have against Melanie? They both worked at Fairhaven, but Tess didn't think they even knew each other very well.

Then, in a flash, something came back to her. A few days ago, Willa had come by the center and passed out a batch of chocolate-chip cookies she'd made. She'd insisted that everyone take one, and Melanie had grudgingly complied. But then she'd gotten that tight-lipped expression she sometimes got, and the moment Willa's back was turned, she dropped her cookie into a nearby trash can. When Tess questioned her about it, Melanie muttered something about strychnine.

"What in the world are you talking about?" Tess had asked.

Melanie shuddered. "The last time I ate something at school that Willa made, I got sick as a dog."

When Tess started to scold her, Melanie grumbled, "Oh, I'm not saying she did it on purpose. But she's not playing with a full deck, Tess. I don't think she should be allowed anywhere near those children, let alone be allowed to administer any medicine. Can you imagine what would happen if she gave the wrong dosage to a child? Or worse, the wrong medication altogether. I've spoken to the director about her, but if something isn't done soon, I may have to take matters into my own hands."

"Tess?"

Her attention snapped back to Willa Banks. The woman stared up at her with an apprehensive expression.

Tess said a little guiltily, "I'm sorry, Miss Willa, but you're wrong about Melanie. We have occasional disagreements just like any other friends, but there's no resentment. We're like sisters. Now, if you'll excuse me, I really have to go. I'm expected at my mother's for dinner.'' She walked around to the side of the truck and opened the door.

"I hope I haven't offended you," Willa said anxiously, following on Tess's heels.

"No, of course not. I'm just in a bit of a hurry."

Willa nodded. "I understand. I won't keep you any longer. Say hello to your mother for me," she called after Tess had climbed into the truck and shut the door.

As she drove away, she glanced in her rearview mirror. Willa remained in the parking lot, staring after her, and an uneasy shiver ran up Tess's backbone.

Where on earth had Willa Banks gotten the notion that Melanie resented Tess?

TESS'S HOME was located down a lonely little tree-shrouded lane about a quarter of a mile from town. She'd chosen the house not so much for the post–World War II bungalow style that she'd always loved, but for the enormous backyard that had come complete with a charming little playhouse and an old-fashioned wooden swing suspended from one of the massive oak trees that shaded the property. Both she and Emily had fallen in love with the place immediately.

And no wonder. The first two years of Emily's life had been spent in a dreary, cramped apartment in Memphis near the university were Tess had both worked and gone to school to complete her degree in business administration. It was the same apartment she'd shared with Alan before he died, and the place was so dark and gloomy with its tiny windows and forest-green carpeting, so bleak with its unhappy memories, that on weekends Tess and Emily had spent much of their time in nearby Overton Park. Emily loved the outdoors, thrived in the fresh air and sunshine, but the crime rate in the park and in the city in general had always worried Tess.

When her mother told her that the Spencers had sold their vacation house on Marvel Lake, Tess had jumped at the chance to come back home. It was ironic, she supposed, that in fleeing the crime in the city, she'd placed her daughter in the most nightmarish danger of all.

Glancing at her home now, Tess wished she could take some comfort in the wide front porch she'd recently painted or in the flower beds she'd carefully tended all summer. But all she could think was that when she went inside, Emily wouldn't be there.

Tess got out of the truck and stood for a moment as memories washed over her. She could almost see Emily sitting on the porch steps, eating an ice-cream cone. Emily on her knees, passionately digging in the dirt as she helped Tess plant impatiens. Emily, playing in the sprinkler. Emily, laughing. Emily, crying. Emily, calling out to her mother in terror…

Grief tightened around Tess's heart as she stared at the house.

She didn't want to go inside. This place, her and Emily's first real home, had once meant so much to her. The house, the yard, even the isolation had become a haven to Tess after a hard day's work, but as she stood in the darkness tonight, a strange, unsettled feeling came over her. This house was no longer her home. No longer a place of solace.

Maybe I should have stayed at Mama's tonight, Tess thought, getting the box of flyers and envelopes from the Explorer. But once she'd gotten to Joelle's, she'd found that she couldn't settle down to dinner or to work, so she'd given up and come home early. Home, but not home.

Letting herself in through the front door, she dropped the heavy boxes on the living-room floor, then walked down the hallway to Emily's bedroom.

Not a day went by that she didn't spend time in her daughter's room. First thing in the morning. Last thing before she went to bed at night. Odd times during the day, when she couldn't seem to function, when she needed to feel a connection with her daughter.

It was dark in the room, but Tess was so familiar with the area that she didn't need a light. She could see the outline of the sleigh bed, the tiny writing desk against one wall, the antique armoire that sat in a corner, doors opened to reveal a formation of Barbies, Beanie Babies, and, on the top shelf, Madam Alexander dolls.

Emily was very particular about the way she arranged her toys, and Tess sometimes wondered if it was practicality or an uncanny perception of life that caused her daughter to put the expensive dolls, the untouchable dolls, out of reach—away from temptation—while she kept the rank-and-file toys on the lower shelves.

Crossing to the window, Tess parted the curtains and stared out at the backyard. The moon was up, casting a sterling light over the grounds and throwing the woods beyond the fence into deep shadow. In the spring, she and Emily picked wildflowers in those woods, and in the fall, wild grapes for jelly. But Tess avoided even looking at the woods much these days. She was too afraid of what might be hidden there.

Turning from the window, she lay down on the bed, smoothing her hand across the pink-and-white coverlet. She could still smell Emily, that sweet, little-girl fragrance that was like sunshine and laughter, and, yes, even tears. But the scent was fading. Tess closed her eyes, trying to get it back.

She reached for Emily's teddy bear, wanting to cuddle it close, the way she wanted to hold her daughter. But the bear, Emily's favorite toy, wasn't in its usual spot on her pillow.

Tess turned on the bedside lamp. Warm light flooded the bedroom, highlighting the armoire where the lifeless eyes of Emily's dolls seemed to gaze back at her.

Uneasiness churned in Tess's stomach. The teddy bear wasn't on the bed or on the floor nearby. Nor had she placed it by mistake with the rest of Emily's toys. It was nowhere to be seen.

And then, very faintly, came an indefinable sound from somewhere deep in the house.

Tess's hand flew to her chest, and in the space of a heartbeat, a million thoughts flew through her head. Someone was in the house with her. Someone had taken Emily's favorite toy. But who? And for God's sake, why?

The noise came again, and the hair at the back of Tess's neck prickled in fear as her mouth went completely dry. Slowly, she got up from the bed and walked out into the hallway, looking first one way and then the other. The living room was at one end of the corridor, her bedroom at the other. For a moment, Tess stood perfectly still, hearing nothing now but the sound of her own heartbeat echoing in her ears.

Had she left the front door unlocked? Her years in the city had made her cautious about such things, but her mind hadn't exactly been working on all cylinders lately.

Slipping out of her shoes, she moved down the hallway on bare feet, peering around the corner into the shadowy living room. Moonlight flooded into the room through the large windows at the front, and Tess searched every corner for anything amiss, some stray movement. Seeing nothing, she hurried across the hardwood floor and checked the bolt on the front door, letting out a breath of relief when she found it locked.

Retracing her steps down the hallway, she flicked on the light in her bedroom, making a quick search of the closet and underneath the bed. By now, she was beginning to relax. The sound she'd heard had either been her imagination or nothing more threatening that settling wood.

Still, she knew she wouldn't rest until she'd checked every room. The bathroom was just past Emily's bedroom, and Tess flipped on the light, her gaze scanning the sink where Emily's toothbrush rested in a Little Mermaid cup. She threw back the shower curtain, revealing Emily's favorite shampoos and soaps, bottled in cartoon-character containers and lined up like little soldiers on a tile ledge above the tub. No one was there, either.

Tess went back out into the hallway. A smaller corridor veered off to the left and led straight back to the kitchen. Something lay curled on the floor where the two hallways connected, and for a moment Tess's breath froze. Not long after they'd moved in, a snake had gotten into the house. It was just a harmless garter snake, but Tess and Emily both had almost gone into hysterics before Tess had calmed herself enough to throw a bath towel over the wriggling serpent and carry it outside.

She stared at the coiled darkness, and seeing no movement, inched toward it. Whatever it was, it didn't appear to be alive, thank goodness.

Then, as she drew closer, recognition shot through her. She bent and almost reverently picked up the frayed burgundy ribbon.

"Mama, Brown Bear's necktie fell off again. Can you fix it for me?"

It was almost as if the question had been spoken aloud, and Tess stood perfectly still, the ribbon clutched in her fist as if it were somehow connected to her daughter. As if, like a divining rod, it could somehow lead her to Emily.

Another sound came from the kitchen, and Tess's knees almost buckled. Hope, as blinding as a spotlight, flooded through her, and without thinking, she tore down the hallway. "Emily? Emily!"

She shoved open the kitchen door and reached for the light switch. "Emily!"

In the bright glare, Tess stood blinking in confusion when she found the kitchen empty. The connection to her daughter was so powerful, the hope so profound, that she'd fully expected to see Emily sitting in her place at the table.

Across the room, the back door stood ajar. Without a moment's hesitation, Tess flung it open and recklessly threw herself down the porch steps. A part of her knew what she was thinking was impossible. A part of her knew it couldn't be true. But she wanted it to be true so badly.

Please let it be Emily, she prayed over and over. *Please let it be Emily.*

"Emily? Is that you, baby? Emily!" *Please, please, please.*

A dog barked somewhere down the street, but no other sound came back to Tess. The silence was almost deafening.

"Emily?" She heard the quiver in her own voice, the edge of desperate hope. "Emily?"

Her gaze scanned the moonlit yard. She moved to the side of the house, her breath coming in painful little spurts. "Emily?" Softer now, more frantic. "Emily?"

The side door to the garage hung open, as if someone had just stepped inside.

Tess's heart stopped, then pounded in double time as the adrenaline began to flow through her veins. She put her hands to her cheeks. Her skin felt clammy, deathly cold. She took a long, measured breath, trying to calm her racing heart. Her panic.

"Emily?"

Entering the garage, Tess reached for the light switch, but then she remembered that the bulb had burned out several days ago and she hadn't gotten around to replacing it. She turned and propped open the door, letting moonlight filter in.

She could make out shadows, indistinct shapes. Bicycles. A lawn mower. A metal rack of paint cans and solvents. At the end of the rack, another shadow, something Tess couldn't quite identify. Then the shadow moved—

And in that instant Tess knew with an almost mind-numbing dread that the eyes staring at her through the darkness were not her daughter's.

Fury overcame her fear. She knew the rational thing to do would be to go inside and call the sheriff's department. But the intruder would be long gone before the police could get there. And Tess knew, beyond a shadow of a doubt, that whoever was in the garage with her had taken Emily. The kidnapper was trapped, cornered. And if he—she—refused to lead Tess to Emily, she would kill him.

"Tell me where my daughter is," she said in a low, feral voice. She hardly recognized the sound of it. "Tell me!"

The shadow seemed to shrink against the wall, to cower as Tess spoke. The knowledge that she had the power to instill fear emboldened her. She reached behind her, plucked a hammer off the wall and slowly moved across the garage toward the shadow.

"I'll kill you," she said. "I swear I'll kill you if you don't tell me where my daughter is."

The shadow moved, just slightly, but Tess froze. Then came the sound of metal scraping on concrete. Tess glanced up. In the darkness, she could barely discern the heavy metal rack as it came crashing toward her.

Chapter Eight

Tess sat on the front-porch steps holding an ice pack to her head.

"Sure you don't want to go to the hospital and have that bump checked out?" Abby Cross plopped down beside Tess on the step and folded her arms over her knees. She and Dave Conyers had arrived shortly after Tess's initial call to the sheriff's station. Lieutenant Conyers was still inside with a team of deputies and forensic technicians, while other officers combed the woods out back.

Tess shook her head. "I'm okay. I appreciate your concern, but I don't want to leave the house. They might find something." She put the ice pack on the porch behind her and tentatively massaged her head with her fingertips. She had a goose egg, but nothing too serious, thanks to her reflexes. She'd jumped out of the way of the metal rack in the nick of time, but she'd fallen in the process, banging her head against the concrete floor of the garage. And the kidnapper had gotten away.

She glanced at Abby. In the muted light from the living-room window, she could see the detective's sober expression. "How much longer will it take?"

"They're almost finished. Hopefully, we'll get lucky, but there's not a lot to go on."

Tess turned back to stare out into the front yard. Police cruisers were parked at the side of the road in front of her house, and she could hear the static transmission from one of the radios. The sound, along with the flashing lights, created a surreal effect in the darkness.

Abby touched her shoulder. "Tess? Are you sure you're okay?"

Tess closed her eyes briefly. "I was so certain it was Emily. I mean, a part of me knew it was impossible, but I couldn't help hoping. I couldn't help thinking that maybe a miracle had happened. Maybe she'd gotten away somehow, and she'd found her way back home to me. It does happen that way sometimes. You hear about stories like that on the news—" Her voice broke, and she turned away. She knew what Abby was thinking. What Tess was thinking herself. You also heard about the stories that didn't turn out so lucky.

She hugged her legs, resting her chin on her knees. "That's why I went out to the garage. I thought when she heard my car pull up, she might have gone running out there to find me. Only—"

"It wasn't Emily," Abby said softly.

Tess swallowed past the lump in her throat, trying to beat back a rising tide of emotion. "I was so *close,*" she whispered. "If I'd seen who was in the garage… If I'd been more careful…we might know where Emily is right now."

"You can't beat yourself up over this, Tess. You did what any mother in your position would have done. You went looking for your child."

Tess's eyes filled with tears. "I just want her to

come home. I just want to find her. Why can't we find her?''

"We're doing everything we can."

She gazed at the sky. "I keep thinking about when she was little. She wasn't an easy baby. She didn't sleep through the night until she was nearly two years old. Sometimes I used to get so exhausted from being up with her that I would have done just about anything for a good night's sleep. Now when I go to bed...the house is so quiet...I'd give anything to go back to that time...to be able to hold her in my arms and rock her..."

"I know."

"I want her to be all right. I want her to be safe. God, you can't imagine the things that go through my head at night."

"I think I can," Abby said.

Tess glanced up at her. "Of course. Sadie. I'd forgotten."

This time it was Abby who turned her gaze to the darkness. "When she first disappeared, I didn't think Naomi would get through it. I thought we were going to lose her, too."

"But she's so strong," Tess said in surprise.

"She's strong because she's had to be," Abby said grimly. "I don't know if you know this or not, but Sadie wasn't the only child Naomi lost."

Tess felt a welling of compassion inside her chest. "She had another child?"

Abby tucked a strand of dark hair behind one ear. "Do you remember the double tornadoes that ripped through here fifteen years ago? Homes, businesses, schools—all destroyed in the space of a heartbeat. Twenty-three people were killed, and I don't know how many more were injured or lost their homes. Jefferson County was declared a disaster area.''

"I remember," Tess said. "Mama woke me up, and we went over to our neighbor's storm cellar. The roof of their house was torn off, just peeled back like the lid on a tin can, but our house right next door was hardly touched.''

"Funny how it happens that way sometimes," Abby mused. "Anyway, my mother and I were gone that night. I was in a basketball tournament down in Jackson, and we got stranded because of the bad weather. Naomi was home alone, and she went into labor. The power and telephone lines were all down, so she had to drive herself to the hospital. The roads were a mess, like a war zone, she said. She had to stop times to clear debris out of the road before she could even get through. By the time she got to the hospital, she was hemorrhaging pretty badly, but they were so short-staffed with all the emergencies, she didn't get treatment right away. She almost died. Her babies—''

Tess caught her breath. "Babies?''

"Sadie was a twin, Tess. The other child, another little girl, died that night.''

"I'm sorry. I didn't know.''

Abby shrugged. "Not many people do. With everything that happened that night, a stillborn baby got lost in all the other tragedies. After a while, hardly anyone remembered, and Naomi has never been able to talk about it.''

"I'm so sorry," Tess said again.

Abby nodded. "I know you are. And I'm not telling you this to try and diminish your loss. I guess what I'm trying to say is that people survive some pretty terrible things. Somehow they find the strength to get through it, and you will, too.''

Tess took a tissue out of her pocket and wiped her eyes. "I'm not sure I want to get through it."

"Just give yourself some time," Abby advised. She paused then said apologetically, "Look, I know you've been over this already with Lieutenant Conyers, but he's asked me to talk to you again. You feel up to going over it one more time? You may remember something else?"

Tess nodded numbly. "Where do you want me to start?"

"At the beginning, when you first got home. You mentioned that you already felt uneasy before you went inside. Think back, Tess. Was there some reason why you felt that way? Something out of the ordinary that you maybe noticed just in passing? A car parked down the road? A window left open in your house? Anything?"

Tess shook her head. "No, there wasn't anything like that. I would have noticed a strange car. My house is the only one on this road. And as for windows—" She shrugged. "I didn't leave any open. And I'm sure my doors were locked. I'm pretty careful about that sort of thing. I don't know how someone got inside."

"There's no sign of a forced entry. Who all has a key to your house?"

"Just my mother and my friend, Melanie Kent."

"Melanie Kent works at Fairhaven, doesn't she?"

Tess nodded. "She's the librarian."

"You two have been friends for a long time, I take it."

"Since we were kids."

Abby paused almost imperceptibly. "According to the statement she gave, Melanie was one of the last people to talk to Emily before she disappeared."

"I guess that's true. She talked to Emily every afternoon. The two of them are very close." Uneasiness prickled at Tess's nerve endings. "Why do you want to know about Melanie?"

Abby met her gaze in the darkness. "I noticed a wheelchair ramp out back. Does she come out here often?"

Anger flared inside Tess. "Melanie loves Emily as if she were her own daughter. If you're insinuating—"

Abby put up a hand. "Take it easy, Tess. I'm not insinuating anything. These questions are purely routine. You know that."

"I'm sorry. It's just—"

"Hard."

Tess nodded miserably. "Every facet of my life has been poked and prodded, and we still don't have a clue who took her. We still don't know where my daughter is."

"Just hang with me a little longer, okay? I know it's difficult, but these questions are important. Now, I want you to think back to when you first went inside the house. Try to picture it in your mind and tell me everything that happened. Just walk me through it."

Tess closed her eyes and did as Abby told her. She recounted in painstaking detail how she'd gone into Emily's bedroom, how she'd heard the noise, found the ribbon, then rushed outside to investigate.

"That's it," she said with a helpless shrug. "That's all I remember."

"You're sure you didn't get a look at the suspect?

Even just a glance. Think hard, Tess. Did you get any kind of impression at all?''

"No," Tess said, clenching her hands into fists. "I wish I had. You don't know how badly I wish I could give you a physical description or something else to go on, but it was too dark in the garage. I didn't see anything."

"You couldn't tell if the suspect was male or female?"

"It could have been anyone." Even someone she knew, Tess thought with a shudder. "All I saw was a shadow at the end of the metal rack."

"All right, just think about that for a minute. Picture the shadow in your mind. Was it tall, short, thin, heavyset?"

"I couldn't tell. It wasn't like a…a silhouette or an outline or anything specific. It was just a shadow, a…darkness. I didn't even know it was a person until I saw movement."

"*How* did it move?" Abby stressed. "Fast? Slow? Toward you? Away from you?"

Tess shook her head helplessly.

"Did the suspect say anything? You didn't hear a voice? What about a smell? Think now. Cologne? Hair spray? Anything like that?"

"No…"

"You don't sound so sure," Abby said sharply. "Did you remember something?"

Tess closed her eyes, conjuring the shadow, that indistinct shape she'd glimpsed seconds before the shelf had tumbled toward her. There had been something else right after she'd fallen. An impression she couldn't quite put her finger on. A sound? A scent? Or was that fleeting memory only her imagination, induced by the blow to her head?

"Tell me," Abby coaxed.

"I'm not sure."

"Tess, it's very important that you not hold anything back."

"I'm not. I just can't remember..."

"Please try."

"I am!" She dropped her head in her hands in frustration. "I know I should have paid more attention, but it all happened so fast, and all I could think about was finding Emily. I don't know if the shadow was tall. I don't know if it was a man or woman. I don't know if there was a scent. The only thing I remember sensing clearly was...fear."

"Your fear?"

Tess shook her head slowly. "The kidnapper's fear. I wanted to kill him, and I think he knew it. I took a hammer down from the wall, and I was prepared to do whatever I had to do to make him tell me where Emily was."

"I believe you," Abby said in a strangely subdued voice. "Nothing is missing from the house besides Emily's teddy bear?"

Tess frowned. "I can't be sure, but I searched through the house when I first heard the noise, and I didn't see anything out of place except for the ribbon. It must have fallen off Emily's bear, and the kidnapper didn't notice."

"That's one possibility."

Tess turned her head, meeting Abby's gaze. "What do you mean?"

Abby hesitated, as if she wanted to say something more but didn't think she should. She gave a brief nod toward the house. "Let's just wait and see if they find anything."

As if on cue, Dave Conyers stuck his head out the front door. "Abby? Can I see you inside?"

Tess started to rise, too, but Abby put a hand on her shoulder. "You stay put. I'll be back in a minute."

Uneasiness gnawed at Tess as she watched the two detectives disappear inside the house. They'd found something. Something bad. Tess was certain of it. That's why Abby hadn't wanted her to follow them inside.

Shivering uncontrollably, Tess got up and walked over to the door. It was slightly ajar and she pushed it open, until she could hear the muted voices of the detectives inside.

"I thought the note was probably a hoax, but now I'm not so sure," Conyers was saying.

"Maybe the kidnapper is sending messages to let her know that Emily is okay," Abby said doubtfully.

Conyers snorted. "Kidnappers aren't usually so considerate. I'll tell you what I think. The son of a bitch is playing head games with her, is what I think. Getting his kicks out of watching her suffer. The kid was probably dead after the first twenty-four hours—"

Tess felt herself go almost completely still except for a buzzing inside her head. "No!"

Both detectives spun toward her, and she saw in a flash the severity of their features, the pity in their eyes. The reality of what they knew on their faces.

Dizziness weakened her legs, and Tess clutched frantically at the door frame. A crushing weight pressed down on her, and she felt as if she were being suffocated. As if she were trapped in some horrible nightmare where she could neither speak nor move. She was paralyzed to help herself or her daughter. All she could think, all she could do was utter the same inane prayer over and over inside her head. *No. Please, no.*

Abby was beside her in seconds. She took Tess's arm, trying to lead her inside. "Just take it easy," she murmured. "Let's get you over to the couch."

Tess mustered the strength to shrug her off. "I don't want to sit. I'm all right." She put a hand to her neck, as if she could somehow claw away the vise that had gripped her by the throat. *Emily! Oh, my baby!*

"Then let's step outside and let you get some air," Abby said.

Tess resisted even that. Her gaze locked with Lieutenant Conyers. "She's not dead. I would know it if she were."

He shuffled uncomfortably under the force of her stare. "Look, we're just exploring every possibility here," he said defensively. "It's our job. We have to face facts—"

"You've thought that all along, haven't you?" Tess demanded. "You never believed you'd find her alive. That's why the search has been scaled down so quickly. That's why the volunteer center is being shut down. You gave up on her right from the first."

"That's not true," Abby said firmly. She took Tess's arms. "Listen to me, Tess. Until we know differently, Emily is alive to us. She will remain alive. Do you understand what I'm saying?"

"I understand what you're saying," Tess said numbly. "But I wonder if you really believe it."

Without another word, she turned and walked back outside. She couldn't listen to them any longer. Couldn't bear to hear the defeat in their voices, to see the pity in their eyes. They thought Emily was dead. They'd thought that all along, but Tess knew better. If Emily was gone, she would know it. She would *feel* it. Emily wasn't lost to her forever. She couldn't be.

"Dear God," she whispered. "Don't let it be true."

Holding back sobs, she stumbled across the front yard toward her truck. As she reached the driveway, a car pulled in behind her Explorer, and headlights caught her in the face. For a moment, she stood frozen, stunned, not able to move for fear she would collapse if she did.

Someone got out of the car. She heard the door slam, and then, as if from a great distance, someone called her name.

But Tess couldn't answer. There was a terrible roaring in her ears, a tightness in her chest that stole her breath. The ground swayed, and as if in slow motion, her legs crumpled beneath her.

JARED CAUGHT HER before she hit the ground. He eased her back carefully on the grass, kneeling beside her. Even in the darkness, he could see the paleness of her face, the fragile look of her features. It was a hot night, but her skin felt cold. Too cold. He wondered if she'd gone into shock.

What on earth had happened to her tonight? He glanced at the police cars parked out front, the lights blazing inside the house. Fear gripped his heart as he stared down at her in the moonlight. "Tess? Tess! Can you hear me?"

Her eyes were closed, but a single tear slipped from the corner of her lashes.

"Tess, talk to me. What's wrong?"

Her head moved back and forth, as if she was in the

throes of some terrible nightmare. "It's not true," she whispered. "It can't be true."

Dread seeped over Jared like a cold, dank fog. "What can't be true? What happened? Is it Emily?" *Please, no,* he silently prayed.

Tess opened her eyes and gazed up at him. For a moment, she seemed unable to focus, then she grabbed his hand, squeezing it hard between her own. "They think she's dead, but she's not. She's not dead, Jared. I would know if she were. Do you understand? I would *know*."

"Tess—" He was helpless to know what to say to her, how to comfort her. The loss of a child was something he couldn't begin to comprehend, and yet the moment he'd spotted the police cars in front of her house, a terrible anguish had seized him. He didn't know the child. She was a stranger to him, but she was Tess's daughter. And there was a time when she might have been his.

Tess struggled to sit up, but Jared tried to ease her back down. "Take it easy, honey."

"I have to find her." Her movements frantic, she clutched at his hands to pull herself up. "I have to go look for her."

They both rose to their feet, and Jared put his hands on her arms to steady her. "Maybe we should go inside—"

"No. No!" She glanced up into his face. "You said you'd help me. You said you'd do anything—"

"I will, but Tess—"

"Then help me find her. Help me look for her."

The desperation in her voice tore at Jared's resolve. He knew that he should back away, let her go, get out of her life. But he could no more ignore her grief and pain than he could have stopped the beating of his heart. Without thinking, he pulled her to him, holding her close. "Tess, Tess."

She cried silently, her tears soaking into his shirt. She was rigid in his arms, unyielding, but she didn't move away. He buried his hand in her hair, holding her against him, trying to offer some comfort. No matter what had happened between them in the past, he couldn't remain immune to her pain, to any mother's pain, at the news that a missing child might never be coming back.

But this wasn't just any mother. This was Tess.

"Please help me find her," she whispered.

"I will." At that moment, Jared didn't think there was anything he wouldn't do for her, but she might be asking the impossible. He closed his eyes, stroking her hair. "I'll help you, Tess. Whatever you want."

She drew back, wiping her face with her hand, and he offered her his handkerchief. She accepted it gratefully, dabbing at her eyes. "She's not dead. Do you believe me?"

"Yes." Then why did he suddenly feel as if his heart had been ripped in two? He swept her hair from her face. "I believe you, but you have to tell me what happened here tonight. I need to know…what to do."

She turned and glanced over her shoulder at the house. "Someone was here."

Her voice was calm now and steady, which chilled him as much as her tears had. "What do you mean, someone was here?"

She turned back to him, her hazel eyes shadowed with…not fear, he thought. Something worse than fear. "Someone was in the house when I got home. He took Emily's teddy bear."

"He? You saw him?"

She shook her head. "He. She. It. The kidnapper."

The hair at the back of Jared's neck stood on end. "Are you saying the kidnapper was *here?* In your house?"

"He took Emily's teddy bear," she said again. "It's her favorite toy. She can't sleep without it. The police think he took it because he's playing mind games with me. They think he did it to torment me because… because Emily's already dead."

The implication hit Jared with the force of a freight train. Someone was deliberately tormenting Tess. Playing mind games, she said. If that was the case, then Emily wasn't the only one in danger.

"Let me see what I can find out," he said grimly. "Will you come back up to the house with me?"

She pulled away from him. "No. I can't go back in there. I can't face them. I don't want to see…what's in their eyes."

"All right," Jared said, reluctant to leave her alone. "Just stand on the front porch and wait for me. Will you do that?" When she hesitated, he tightened his grip on her arms. "Please. Just wait for me. Then I'll go with you. We'll go look for Emily together. Wherever you want to go."

"You're only doing it to humor me," she said softly. "But I don't care. I don't want to be alone. Not to-night."

Jared wanted nothing more than to put his arms around her again, to tell her she never had to be alone. But that might be yet another promise he couldn't keep.

SERGEANT CROSS WAS with a group of cops huddled in the living room, but Jared didn't wait to be noticed.

He strode over to where she stood and took her arm. "Sergeant Cross? May I have a word with you?"

Her startled glance went from his face to his hand on her arm and then slowly back up to his face. Very deliberately she removed her arm from his grasp. "Mr. Spencer, isn't it? The governor's friend?"

One of the cops snickered, but Jared ignored him. "I need to talk to you."

"Hey, Abby, new boyfriend?" one of the deputies jeered.

"At least this one doesn't have one foot in the grave," someone else piped in. "And he looks like he's got money to boot. That your Jaguar parked out in the driveway?"

The first cop whistled. "Jaguar, huh? Burke's not going to like that competition."

"Oh, shut up," Sergeant Cross snapped. "Sam Burke could teach you all a thing or two."

"I'll bet he's taught *you* a thing or two!"

She spared Jared a killing look, as if to chide him for what he'd started. "As you can see, I'm busy at the moment. If you want to wait outside, I'll come look for you when I'm finished."

"It'll only take a minute. Please," he added in a barely conciliatory tone.

She shoved her hair behind her ears and moved past him. Someone made another joke as she walked away, and Jared could see that she was clearly annoyed.

"You always have to put up with that kind of attitude?" he asked her.

She shrugged. "Goes with the territory. Now, what is it I can do for you, Mr. Spencer? And make it fast. You shouldn't even be in here. This is a police investigation."

"That's exactly why I'm here. I just left Tess outside. She's a wreck." He glanced down the hall to where yet another cop was dusting for fingerprints on a brass doorknob. "She said someone broke in here tonight. She thinks it was Emily's kidnapper."

Sergeant Cross's lips thinned. "She could have been seriously hurt, but she got lucky—"

A cold chill shot through Jared. "Wait a minute. Are you saying she was attacked?"

"She didn't tell you?"

He swore viciously, then, catching himself, mumbled an apology.

Sergeant Cross shrugged. "I've heard worse, believe me. Look, I shouldn't even be talking to you about this, but you said you were a friend of Tess's, and I think she could use one right now. According to Tess, she got home around nine tonight and went straight back to her daughter's bedroom. About the same time she noticed a teddy bear missing from the bed she heard a strange noise somewhere in the house. When she went to investigate, she found a ribbon on the floor that had fallen off the bear. She thought Emily had come home. She went tearing off outside to find her."

Jared could picture the scene all too clearly. Tess searching frantically through the house. Calling to Emily. Wanting desperately to believe a miracle had happened, but knowing, deep down inside, that miracles rarely happened.

"When she got outside," Sergeant Cross continued, "she noticed that the side door of the garage was open. She couldn't turn on the light in the garage, though, because the bulb was burned out. So she propped open the door and—"

"He was in there." Jared's hand clenched into fists at his sides.

Sergeant Cross's gaze met his and she nodded. "She saw something move. A shadow, she says. So she armed herself with a hammer and went after him."

"Damn." Jared plowed his fingers through his hair as images strobed through his head. "She could have been killed."

"Like I said, she got lucky. The suspect pushed over a heavy metal rack that held some paint cans and solvents, but Tess managed to jump out of the way in time. She could have been crushed."

Jared exhaled slowly, trying to control a sudden, wild surge of anger. "Who was it?"

"That's what we're trying to find out."

"Do you think it was Emily's kidnapper?"

Sergeant Cross hesitated. "I don't know."

Jared frowned. "What do you mean, you don't know? Who else could it have been?"

She shrugged. "We're just going to have to wait and see where the evidence takes us."

"*Wait?*" Jared said angrily. "Seems to me there's been enough of that. Why the hell aren't you out trying to find this guy?"

She bristled slightly under his attack, but, except for a faint red bloom on her cheeks, she held her cool. "We're doing everything we can. We've got deputies out right now, canvassing the area, talking to the nearest neighbors to see if anyone might have seen something suspicious around here tonight, but given the isolation of this place, it's doubtful we'll find any witnesses."

It didn't surprise Jared that Tess had chosen a place so remote. She'd always been something of a loner. He thought about what she'd said earlier, when he'd told her he would help her look for Emily. *"You're only doing it to humor me. But I don't care. I don't want to be alone. Not tonight."* Had she changed in six years?

His gaze went back to Sergeant Cross. "I'm sure you're going through the motions," he said. "But I have to wonder if your heart is really in it. Tess says you think Emily is already dead."

The flush on Sergeant Cross's cheeks deepened, and her dark eyes glittered with anger. "I'll tell you exactly what I told Tess. Emily is alive to me, to all of us, until we find out differently. That's how we've proceeded with this investigation from the first, and that's how we'll continue to operate. You understand?"

"I understand that Tess is in a lot of pain right now," he said harshly. "And there doesn't seem to be anything anyone can do about it."

"We're all in a lot of pain, Mr. Spencer. This isn't just Tess's loss. Emily is one of Eden's children. Everyone in this town takes her disappearance personally. If you think differently, then you don't know much about us." There was a faint note of challenge in Sergeant Cross's voice. She wasn't a large woman, only about five-six or so, slender, attractive. Very feminine in spite of the badge clipped to her jeans and the shoulder holster she wore underneath her jacket.

At six-two, Jared towered over her, and he wasn't above using his size, his gender, or even his connections to bully her. He wasn't above bringing the full weight of the Spencer name to bear against her if he thought it would do any good. He'd made enemies in the last six years, and he'd make another one in a heartbeat if he had to. But with Abby Cross he held back.

Something in her eyes, a terrible wisdom, made him realize that her words were not just a hollow sentiment. Her job hadn't anesthetized her to pain and compassion. She felt for Tess. And for Emily.

"We've done everything we can to find Emily," she said again. "Most of us on this case have been working fifteen and sixteen hours a day. We've examined every lead, conducted countless interviews, studied what little evidence we've been able to gather from every conceivable angle. We've left no stone unturned, Mr. Spencer, which is why I'm going to ask you this— What exactly is the nature of your relationship with Tess Campbell?"

Suddenly the compassion fled, replaced by a cold, calculating scrutiny. The dark eyes narrowed on him, and Jared felt a flare of anger, a faint sense of betrayal. She was good, he thought. He hadn't even seen her ambush coming.

"I told you. We're friends."

"Friendship encompasses a range of relationships. Could you be a little more specific?"

"We were lovers once," he said flatly. "Is that specific enough for you?"

She seemed unfazed by the revelation. "When was this?"

"Six years ago."

"The relationship was serious?"

Jared shrugged. "For me it was."

"And Tess?"

"You'd have to ask her."

"I may just do that," Sergeant Cross said. "I wonder why she never mentioned you when we questioned her about relationships past or present."

"Maybe she didn't think it was important enough,"

Jared said. "It was a long time ago. Maybe she forgot."

Sergeant Cross's dark gaze flickered over him, then moved back up to his face. "Somehow I doubt that," she murmured. "Who broke off the relationship?"

"She did."

"Do you mind telling me what happened?"

Yes, Jared thought. *I mind a great deal.* "She said we were too different. We weren't meant to be together. It never would have worked out."

"Did you agree with her?"

"Eventually." But it had taken a long time. And even now, seeing Tess again, had raised some of the old questions. Some of the old emotions. And yes, even some of the old resentment. He'd loved Tess unconditionally. He'd wanted to marry her and live happily ever after with her, but she'd wanted a relationship only on her terms. She hadn't wanted him for who he was, but in spite of it.

"You sound a little bitter," Sergeant Cross observed.

Jared tried to keep his expression neutral as he gazed down at her. "If I were bitter, I wouldn't be here trying to help her, would I?"

"That all depends, I guess."

Uneasy fingers crept up Jared's spine. "Wait a minute." He started to take her arm, then thought better of it. "You don't think I'm the one who broke into Tess's house tonight? You don't think I had anything to do with her daughter's disappearance?"

Something flickered in Sergeant Cross's brown eyes. "It's like I said, we're leaving no stone unturned."

"I don't believe this," Jared raged. "You've got some psycho breaking into Tess's house, taking one of her daughter's toys, maybe coming after Tess next. And what are you doing about it? You stand here questioning me.''

"Take it easy, Mr. Spencer. These questions are routine. Don't take it personally."

"It's hard not to." Her calm, slightly disapproving voice made Jared feel like an idiot for his outburst. Made him feel guilty for something he hadn't even done. Oh, she was good all right. Very damn good.

"Just a couple more questions," she said. "Do you know of anyone who might carry a grudge against Tess? Who might want to hurt her? And I'm not talking about physically. I'm talking emotionally."

The worst kind of torture, Jared thought. Taking a woman's child. Someone who would do that had a truly twisted mind. He had an urgent need, suddenly, to rush outside and make sure Tess was still there. Make sure she was okay. "Like I said, we knew each other six years ago, but even then I didn't really know any of her friends or acquaintances. We kept pretty much to ourselves."

"Why was that?"

"It was the way Tess wanted it."

"What about now? Do you know of anyone who might have it in for her?"

Jared shook his head. "That I couldn't tell you. Until yesterday, I hadn't seen her in six years."

Sergeant Cross's eyebrows lifted slightly. "Really? Because you seem awfully concerned for Tess's welfare for someone who hasn't seen her in so long."

"Her daughter is missing, Sergeant Cross. I'd have to be pretty hard-hearted not to be concerned."

She looked as if she wanted to challenge his assertion, but instead she shrugged. "Well, thanks for your cooperation, Mr. Spencer. If anything else comes up, where can I get in touch with you?''

He fished a business card out of his pocket and handed it to her. She studied it for a moment, then glanced up. ''You're *that* Spencer? The Spencer Hotels Spencer? I had no idea.''

''Didn't I tell you that earlier?'' Jared asked.

''You didn't mention it, no, except to threaten to bring in the governor. Now that I know who you are, that threat seems a little less amusing,'' she said dryly.

''It wasn't an idle threat,'' Jared said. ''Governor Denton is my godfather. If I thought this case was being mishandled, I wouldn't hesitate to call him.''

Sergeant Cross folded her arms. ''Do yourself a favor, Mr. Spencer, and stay out of this investigation. Don't call the governor.''

''Don't give me cause to.''

They stared at each other for a moment longer before Jared turned to leave.

''Mr. Spencer?''

He stopped at the door and glanced over his shoulder.

''One last thing. Where were you at nine o'clock tonight?''

Chapter Nine

Tess turned with an anxious glance when Jared stepped outside. She stood at the porch railing, one hand clutching a newel post for support. Jared didn't think she'd moved a muscle since he'd left her a few minutes earlier.

"What did you find out?"

"Nothing more than you'd already told me." He glanced back at the house. "I think they're almost finished. If you still want to go out to search for Emily, I'll take you."

She hugged her arms to herself, looking exhausted in the dim illumination from the window. "I know you probably think I'm crazy, but I have to do something. I can't stay here all tonight, pacing the floor. Thinking...what I know I'll be thinking. I can't be here safe and comfortable while she's out there somewhere."

His heart turned over at the look on her face. "I understand."

As if overcome by weariness, she turned and leaned her head against the post, gazing out across the yard. "Sometimes I still can't believe this is happening."

Jared came up behind her and put his hands on her shoulders. For a split second she tensed, but then, unexpectedly, she relaxed against him. He closed his eyes, wanting to pull her close but knowing that he shouldn't. That he didn't dare. The instinct to protect her had never been stronger in him, but there was danger in trying to rescue Tess. She'd rejected him once, broken his heart, and it had taken him a long time to get over it. He would be a fool to think that, in six years, anything had changed between them.

But something had changed. Her daughter was missing, and somehow Tess's tragedy, her loss, had diminished the past, made the differences that still existed between them insignificant. Emily's disappearance put so many things into perspective, at least for Jared.

Almost against his will, he leaned slightly into Tess, skimming his lips across her hair so softly he didn't think she'd be able to feel his touch. "I'm sorry you're having to go through this."

She drew a ragged breath. "It's not about me. It's about Emily. What *she's* having to go through. I just keep seeing her..."

She didn't finish the thought, but Jared knew what she meant. The same images had been flitting through his head all evening. That innocent face he'd seen in the paper, that precious child so still and silent. Those dark eyes closed forever.

"Did you mean what you said earlier?" he asked in a soft, fierce voice. "That you'd know if Emily were dead? You'd feel it?"

She turned and gazed up at him, her eyes flooding with tears. "Yes."

His grasp tightened on her arms. "Then that's what you have to hang on to. That's what you have to believe."

"Jared—" Something swept across her face, an

emotion so raw it took his breath away. It was almost as if she was reaching out to him, trying to connect with him in a way only the two of them could share.

But it was a fleeting feeling, because the front door opened, jarring the moment, and they both turned as Sergeant Cross came outside. Jared dropped his hands from Tess's arms and took a slight step away from her.

The move was not lost on Sergeant Cross. Her dark gaze flickered over him. "Lieutenant Conyers is posting a deputy outside here for the rest of the night." She put a hand on Tess's arm. "But maybe you should think about spending the night at your mother's house anyway. Even with a deputy out here, this place is pretty isolated."

"I'll be all right." But Tess didn't look all right. Her features were pale and fragile in the filtered light, and Jared had that urge again, that almost overpowering need to take care of her, to make things right for her. He was a Spencer. He should be able to fix this. But how could he? Her child was missing, and if Emily wasn't found soon, no amount of money or power in the world would ever make things right for her again.

"I'll be in touch if there's any news," Sergeant Cross told them as she hurried down the porch steps. At the bottom, she turned to gaze up at them. "Tess, do you remember the profiler who worked on the Sara Beth Brodie case?" When Tess nodded, she said, "He'll be back in town in a day or two. Would you be willing to talk to him again?"

"If you think it would help."

"I think it might. At any rate, I'd like to get his input." She glanced at Jared. "I guess I'll see you around, Mr. Spencer."

He gave her a brief nod. "Good night, Sergeant Cross."

Several minutes later, the rest of the police personnel had cleared out, too. In the silence that followed their departure, a strange uneasiness settled over the porch, as if alone, Tess and Jared didn't quite know what to say to each other. How to react to one another. They remained on the porch for several more minutes, while across the street a deputy sat watching them from his patrol car. Had Sergeant Cross briefed him on her earlier conversation with Jared?

"Where were you at nine o'clock tonight?"

"On the road. I left Jackson around seven-thirty."

"Alone?"

"Yes, alone."

Which meant, of course, that he couldn't prove his whereabouts.

It was disturbing, to say the least, that in wandering back into Tess's life, he'd suddenly become a suspect in the worst kind of crime.

"I should lock up the house before we go," Tess murmured. Her gaze slid to the door, and in the murky light, Jared saw her shiver.

"I can do it," he said. "Just tell me where your keys are."

"At least let me come inside with you," he said when she hesitated.

She nodded, and they entered the house together. Jared watched her as she moved around the room, running her hand across the back of the sofa, the surface of a table, as if she was trying to reacquaint herself with a place that she'd once been familiar with. A place that had once been her home. Now she seemed strangely out of place here, even to Jared.

She left the living room to check the back door, and while she was gone, Jared glanced around, taking in the details of the room that he'd missed earlier. The soft, earthy shades, the polished floors, the framed pictures of Emily almost everywhere he looked. It was a nice home, he thought. Cheerful. Comfortable. Under different circumstances, the muted color scheme might even have been peaceful. But the subdued decor struck him as a little off kilter now, maybe because it didn't reflect the upheaval in Tess's life, the tragedy that had made her one of the walking wounded.

She came slowly down the hallway, still dressed in the same jeans and cotton shirt she'd had on earlier. Her appearance—the weight loss, the haunted expression, the dark shadows under her eyes—was a grim reminder of all that she'd gone through.

"I'm ready." Her gaze darted about the room as if she was afraid the intruder still lurked behind the furniture.

"Let's go then." Outside, he waited for her to lock the front door, then he took her elbow and guided her down the porch steps. They crossed the yard to his car, and Jared helped her inside.

As he moved around to the driver's side, his gaze scanned the darkness. He couldn't shake the feeling that someone, other than the deputy, watched them from the shadows. The idea that Tess could be the target of a twisted mind, someone demented enough to have kidnapped her daughter and then returned time and again to torment her scared Jared half to death. What if the police couldn't protect her? Would she let him take over? Would she let him do whatever was necessary to insure her safety?

Not if she was anything like the Tess he used to

know. That Tess would have fought him tooth and nail. The suggestion that she couldn't take care of herself would have been galling to her.

But she'd asked for his help tonight. She'd told him she didn't want to be alone. Jared didn't want to read too much into her actions, but he couldn't help wondering if she was finally coming around to trusting him in a way she'd never been able to before.

He climbed inside the car, started the engine, then backed out of the driveway. He drove slowly, heading for the main highway as Tess sat on the edge of her seat, her eyes peeled on the sliding scenery. The moon was up, but the woods along the road blotted much of the light. It would be next to impossible to see anything in those trees, but Jared kept driving. They didn't talk. Tess barely moved. After a while, he realized she'd done this before, probably every single night since Emily had gone missing, and it tore at his heart to think of her out here alone, searching for her daughter.

You don't have to be alone, he wanted to tell her, but who was he to make that promise? She'd left him once. She'd made her feelings clear back then. And Jared had accepted her decision. In time, he'd gotten over the hurt and bitterness, and he'd made a life for himself in New Orleans. A good life. He'd followed the blueprint that had been mapped out for him since birth, and he'd been ruthless in his pursuits. He'd set out to make a name for himself in the company, and he had, no matter who he'd had to use in the process. He'd told himself he would no longer live in the past, and he hadn't, no matter what his resolve had cost him. But most of all, he'd given himself permission to embrace his own ambition, to enjoy the fruits of his labor, to be unashamed of who he was and where he'd come from. In looking back, he'd come to realize that his name was a barrier that Tess, not he, had put between them.

Her pride had been formidable back then, and he suspected her resentment had run a lot deeper than either of them ever thought. That was why she'd constantly challenged him.

So why was he here with her now?

The answer was devastatingly simple. Because in a lot of ways, the last six years had been the loneliest of his life. And because Tess needed him. Maybe she'd always needed him, she'd just been too stubborn to .admit it.

He glanced at her now, so quiet and so sad, and he knew that in spite of all that lay between them, he would do anything to take away her pain, to give her back the spark that had made her at once infuriating and irresistible. He could give her anything that money could buy, but he couldn't give her a miracle. He couldn't give her back her daughter.

And the thought of that left him feeling helpless and angry.

THEY DROVE FOR HOURS. Along the highway. Down country roads. Around the lake. Just after midnight, Jared crossed over the bridge on Lake Shore Drive, and they found themselves in Mount Ida, a depressed neighborhood on the south side of town. Even here, where danger lurked around almost every corner, Jared drove aimlessly, turning onto side streets at random. They weren't going to find anything. He knew that. It had been nearly three weeks since Emily disappeared. She could be anywhere, out of the country even, but still he drove on.

As for Tess, he doubted she had any illusions about their search, either. But if he took her home, she wouldn't be able to sleep. She would sit in her house alone, consumed with images of her daughter, playing that terrible game of what-if. If he could make even a few hours easier for her, then so be it.

The night was warm and muggy, and Jared had been driving with the air conditioner on. When he saw Tess shiver, he turned it off and rolled down his window. They were in downtown Eden now, and as they moved along the narrow streets, he was struck by the mood of the town. It was late. Even under normal circumstances the streets would be quiet, all the children long since . home and in bed. But tonight there was a deserted feel to the place, an almost surreal air that hung over the storefronts and restaurants and even the churches.

Emily was everywhere. Her picture stared at them from store windows and from light poles, and messages spelled out on business signs proclaimed a town's unified agony: *We love you, Emily.*

And still Tess said nothing. She watched the darkness with a quiet alertness that was heartbreaking.

"Tess?"

She jumped slightly as if she'd forgotten he was in the car with her. When she turned to face him, he said softly, "Shall I keep driving?"

She nodded and turned back to the window.

He let another few seconds go by, and then, still softly, "Tell me about Emily."

He wasn't sure how she would react to his request, but to his surprise, she gave him a tentative smile. "She's one of the special ones. I know every parent thinks that, but with Emily—" She broke off, leaning back against the seat, staring out the windshield. "It's hard to explain, but you'd know what I mean if you met her. She has this quality about her. It's like she has a light shining on her wherever she goes. She makes you feel humble."

Jared nodded, his throat suddenly tight. When he stopped at a streetlight, Emily's image stared down at him from a light pole. "She's a beautiful child, Tess."

Her eyes glistened in the light from the dash. "You used the present tense."

"I beg your pardon?"

"So many people talk about her in the past tense. She *was* a beautiful child. She *had* this quality about her. I can't tell you how much that hurts. But…you didn't." Her gaze on him intensified. "You believe she's still alive, too, don't you?"

"Yes," he said quietly. "I do."

"Thank you," she whispered. She reached over and covered his hand with hers. He lifted his hand from the steering wheel, and their fingers automatically curled together. Jared felt something stir inside him at the contact, a flicker of warmth that took hold and began to spread.

Their grasp tightened and before he had time to wonder how she might react, he drew their linked hands to his lips. She stiffened slightly as his mouth grazed across her knuckles, but she didn't pull her hand away. Her gaze on him was wide and shimmering, and Jared knew at that moment that he had been kidding himself all these years. He hadn't gotten over Tess Granger. She was still in his blood, and he wondered, with an almost fatalistic yearning, if she always would be.

"Tell me about your life," he said in a low, urgent voice. "The last six years. Tell me about the man you married."

She looked at once startled and wary, and she turned quickly back to the window. "Why would you want to know about Alan?"

"Because I have to know." He rubbed the back of his neck with his hand. "Just talk to me, Tess. About anything. Tell me how you met him."

She shrugged almost imperceptibly. "I moved to Memphis when I left here. He lived in the apartment next to mine."

"Was it love at first sight?" When she didn't answer, Jared said almost angrily, "I guess it had to be. Otherwise, you wouldn't have been so quick to marry him. Unless, of course, you were pregnant."

TESS'S HAND FLEW to her heart as she whirled to face him. She could feel the color drain from her face. "*Pregnant?* Why would you think that?"

"It happens," he said with a shrug, but his gaze on her narrowed. "Two people meet, they get involved. Things get out of hand. They get careless."

"You and I were never careless," she said quickly.

This time it was he who looked startled. "I'm not talking about us. I'm talking about you and…" He trailed off, as if unable to bring himself to say her husband's name. "So is that it? Is that why you married him so quickly? You were pregnant with Emily?"

Oh, God, Tess thought. *Oh, God, oh, God, oh, God!* A part of her had always worried this time would come, but not now. She wasn't ready for it. She didn't know if she had the strength to make Jared understand, to make him believe that if Emily was found, her life could still be in danger from someone in his own family. That in finding out Emily was his daughter, Tess's secret would have to become his. It was a lot to ask of anyone. She clasped her hands in her lap and turned back to the window. "I don't want to talk about this."

"No, I know you don't. You've made it abundantly clear that you don't want to talk about the past. Period. And you know what? I've been asking myself why. What are you hiding, Tess? What are you so afraid of?"

"Nothing!" She put trembling fingertips to her lips, trying to quell her terror. "I just don't see why it matters anymore. Can't you let it go?"

"No," he said grimly, "I can't. I have a right to know why you left town that summer."

"For God's sake, you know why!" she cried angrily.

"Which brings us back to that fateful night. Why, Tess? Why did you do it? Why did you steal my mother's bracelet?"

"I didn't!" she blurted, then almost immediately, she realized her mistake. Her breath left her as their gazes locked in the darkness, and she saw confusion flicker in his eyes. Then anger.

Very deliberately, he pulled to the side of the road and parked the car. The night was silent, except for the ticking of the car engine, the faint hum of an air conditioner somewhere nearby. And the beat of Tess's heart in her ears. The sound was almost deafening.

Jared shifted in his seat to face her. "What did you mean, you didn't steal the bracelet?" When she didn't turn, he took her arms and swung her around. "Answer me, damn it!"

"It doesn't matter," she said with a desperate edge to her voice.

"Like hell it doesn't." His grasp on her arm tightened, and she winced. His grip loosened immediately, but he didn't release her. "Tell me once and for all. Did you steal my mother's bracelet that night?"

She closed her eyes. "No."

"Then for God's sake, why did you let me think that you had?"

She stared up into his dark eyes, resisting the urge to lift her hand, to caress his cheek, to pull his mouth down to hers and make the horror of the last three weeks go away. But it wouldn't go away. Nothing would take away the nightmares until Emily came back home. And if she told Jared the truth, there could be more nightmares.

"Why, Tess?" He gave her arm a little shake.

She drew a trembling breath. "Because it was the only way. You wouldn't have let me go."

"Let you go?" He stared at her incredulously. "You couldn't have just told me the simple truth? That you didn't love me anymore?"

"I couldn't have told you that and made you believe it," she said quietly.

His gaze on her deepened. "Why not?"

She did touch him then, briefly, one fingertip whispering across his lips. "Don't make me say it."

His eyes closed briefly at her touch, but then he seemed to harden his resolve. He stared down at her angrily. "Say what? That you still loved me when you left? Did you?"

"Yes."

He slumped back, letting his head fall against the seat. "Then why didn't you tell me? Why didn't you trust me?"

"I was scared. I didn't want to go to prison. Your father made me a deal and I took it."

"What did he say to you?" Jared said harshly. "What could he possibly have said to make you confess to a crime you didn't commit?"

"He…said that he knew the two of us had been

seeing each other, and he didn't approve. He said you had an important future ahead of you, and I would just hold you back. And he was right, Jared. We were never meant to be together. You know that.''

He turned his head on the seat, staring at her in the darkness. ''You kept saying that until you made yourself believe it,'' he said bitterly.

''Maybe. But there was a lot of truth in his words. Look at all you've accomplished. Look at what you've become. At the age of thirty, you're president of the Spencer Hotels Corporation. It's what you always wanted. Do you honestly believe it would have happened if you'd married me?''

''We'll never know, will we?''

''I didn't want you to have to choose,'' she said softly.

He gave her a hard glance. ''No,'' he said. ''That's not true. You didn't trust me to make the right choice. Isn't that the real reason you left?''

''That was part of it,'' she admitted. ''But can you honestly say you would have given it all up for me if it had come down to a choice?''

''In a heartbeat.'' His gaze met hers in the darkened car, and Tess felt a shiver go through her at his look, at his words. She wanted to reach out and touch him, but she didn't dare.

He stared out the windshield, his features rigidly set. ''My father was always the great manipulator. He always did whatever it took to get what he wanted. He encouraged the competition between Royce and me so that we'd become the kind of men he wanted. He put impossible expectations on us so that we would work even harder for his approval. I went along with it all because I thought it was what I was supposed to do. I made the highest grades, joined the right clubs, did everything the good son was supposed to do, and now I'm sitting here wondering why. What the point of it all was.''

"Jared—"

He turned to face her. "I let you go that night. I knew you weren't capable of stealing that bracelet. I knew something was wrong, but I let you go because—"

"I gave you no choice."

"No," he said. "Because in some ways it was easier to let you go. You wanted our relationship on your terms, Tess. You wanted me to disavow everything I'd been raised to believe in, to want. You were constantly challenging me, doubting me. You never trusted me. You never trusted in *us.* You were never an easy woman to love, but getting over you was the hardest thing I ever had to do."

She wiped a tear from her eyes with her fingertip. "But you did get over me. And all this happened in the past. None of it matters anymore."

"It matters to me." His gaze on her hardened again. "There's still the matter of the bracelet. If you didn't steal it, who did? Who were you protecting that night?"

His accusation shocked her. "What?"

"My father made you a deal. If you left town, stopped seeing me, he'd drop the charges. But if you were innocent, why were you so frightened? It wasn't like you to give up without a fight. Why were you so anxious to accept his terms? You must have been protecting someone, and the only one I can think of who had access to the house—"

Tess gasped in outrage. "If you think my mother capable of such a crime, then you're wrong! Dead wrong! She's the most honest, decent woman I've ever known.''

''Then who?''

When Tess didn't answer, he said roughly, ''You may as well tell me, because I'll find out the truth. One way or another.''

She whirled in her seat, putting her hands on his arms. ''Why can't you just leave it alone?''

''Because I can't.''

''Please, Jared,'' she said desperately. ''If you start asking questions about that night—''

''What?'' He put his hands on her arms, too, and they stared at each for a long, tense moment. ''You're trembling.'' She tried to shrink away from him, but he wouldn't let her. ''Why are you still so afraid?''

His face was close to hers, so close she could see the spark of anger in his eyes, the stubborn line of his jaw and chin, the rigid curve of his mouth. But she could see beyond the grim set of his features, could remember in shocking detail the desire that had once emanated from those same eyes. The way that same mouth had once felt against hers. The way he'd held her…the things he'd whispered to her in the dead of night, in the heat of passion.

And then suddenly, something changed. The anger seemed to drain out of him, and another emotion flickered in his eyes, one that Tess couldn't quite define. Not passion. Not love. But a divination. A sudden knowing that seemed to astound him.

His gaze on her sharpened. ''Tell me,'' he demanded.

''I've told you everything I can. Please don't ask me any more questions.'' Tess opened the door and stumbled outside, suddenly unable to breathe.

He knows, she thought desperately. *He knows about Emily.*

She looked up, and it almost seemed an omen to her that they were parked in front of Fairhaven Academy. The place where Emily had disappeared. Without knowing why, Tess started walking toward the playground. Behind her, she heard Jared get out of the car. He caught up with her and took her arm.

"You can't run away from me this time, Tess. It's not going to be that easy."

You think it was easy six years ago? she wanted to lash out at him, but the resistance had all drained out of her. She couldn't fight him any longer. She didn't have the strength.

Tears streaming down her face, she tried to turn away from him, but he held her still, thumbing away the wetness on her face with a touch so gentle Tess felt everything inside her go still.

"This isn't over, you know. I'm not going away until I find out the truth."

"Do you remember what you said this morning?" she asked quietly. "You said that in light of everything that's happened, you can understand why the past would seem trivial to me."

"I remember."

"Finding Emily is all that matters to me," she said fiercely. "That's all I can think about right now."

"It's all that matters to me, too," he said, his gaze on her deep and probing. "But when we do find her, when we bring her home, I'll be back for some answers. And I warn you, Tess. If you run away, I'll come and find you this time. Count on it."

"THIS IS WHERE she disappeared," Tess said a few minutes later as they walked across the playground together.

"She was out here playing with some of the other students whose parents were late picking them up."

"Why did you decide to send her to Fairhaven?" Jared asked. "Why a private school?"

Tess shrugged. "Because I wanted her to have the best. The tuition was a struggle, and for a while, I wasn't certain she'd be accepted. But there was an unexpected opening and she got in, and...I thought she'd be safe here—" She broke off, her gaze scanning the schoolyard as she fought the demons inside her. As she tried to control the guilt that Jared suspected was tearing her up inside.

"A teacher from each grade is assigned every afternoon to watch the playground, but that day, for some reason, there were more students than usual. One of the teachers remembers seeing Emily on the swing, another on the slide. Some of her friends said she played on the merry-go-round, but no one remembers seeing her leave the playground. No one saw anything suspicious that day. It was as if she vanished into thin air."

Tess sat down in one of the swings and pushed herself to and fro. Her head was bent, and in the darkness she might have passed for a child herself, Jared thought, watching her. She was so thin. So frail. So vulnerable. Whatever she'd done in the past, whatever mistakes she'd made, whatever she'd kept from him, she'd paid, and paid dearly. The last three weeks had been hell on earth for her. He only had to look into her eyes to see the depth of her suffering.

He glanced around the darkened playground. Like a lot of schools, Fairhaven took on a deserted and slightly spooky air at night. The landscaped grounds were shrouded with shadow, and the big, ivy-covered building loomed in the background. A stray breeze moved one of the swings, and ghost laughter seemed to echo across the yard.

A chill swept up Jared's backbone. He closed his eyes, trying to picture the scene as it had unfolded on that day. The children, laughing and playing, oblivious to the danger that lurked nearby. He conjured Emily's image, the dark eyes and hair, that sweet, beautiful face. He put her with the other children, and when he opened his eyes, he could almost see her on the playground.

He watched her climb into one of the swings and pump her little legs furiously until she was flying through the air, shrieking with delight. She had on the school uniform she wore in most of the pictures he'd seen—navy shorts, white short-sleeve shirt. Her dark hair was pulled back and fastened with a red ribbon. She looked sweet and innocent, the way Jared knew she would.

He watched her leave the swing and skip over to the slide. She climbed the steps, and then, arms spread wide, she zoomed toward the ground. At the bottom, she scrambled off the slide and ran, laughing, toward the merry-go-round. Then suddenly, her attention was caught by something. Jared saw her lift her head, as if someone had called to her.

She got off the merry-go-round and started walking slowly away, her form growing more and more indistinct until he could barely see her.

When she'd disappeared altogether, Jared lifted his hand and wiped the moisture from his eyes.

EMILY SNUGGLED Brown Bear in her arms as she stared into the darkness. She'd been so surprised and so happy earlier when she'd come out of the bathroom to find

him on the bed. She'd rushed over and grabbed up the
toy, holding him close.

"Is Mama here?" she'd asked hopefully.

"No, not yet. But soon…"

And then the door closed, and Emily was left alone
again. All alone.

But soon Mama would be here.

More than anything in the world, Emily wanted to
believe that her mother really was coming for her, but
deep down inside, she didn't think it was true. Mama
wasn't coming soon. She might not ever come.

Slipping off the bed, Emily crept across the room to
the door, trying very hard not to make a sound. She
turned the knob, but the door was locked, just as it
always was. Just as she knew it would be. She put her
ear to the door, listening intently. Hearing no sound,
she turned away.

The only window in the room was so high off the
floor that she couldn't look out, even if she stood on
her tippy-toes. But a plastic bench had been placed in
the bathroom for her to use when she had to go potty.
Emily didn't really need the little blue footstool because she was tall enough to go without it, but she
didn't say anything because she didn't want it to be
taken away.

As she had before, she carried the footstool over to
the window and climbed up on it so that she could see
out. There were no other houses around, no lights, just
lots and lots of trees, and in the distance, the sparkle
of water. It made Emily think of the time her mama
had taken her on a picnic by the lake.

Sometimes Emily could hardly remember what
Mama looked like. She squeezed her eyes closed, trying to conjure her mother's image. The long hair, the
pretty smile…

She kept that picture in her mind for as long as she could, and when she finally opened her eyes, the moon was rising over the treetops. That made her think of Mama, too.

Sometimes at home, she and Mama would gaze out the window together, and Mama would tell her stories about the lady who lived on the moon and the diamond necklace she strung from stars.

Sometimes she'd tell Emily the story of the lady trapped in a tower, and the prince who'd climbed up her long, braided hair to rescue her.

"Your hair looks just like hers," Emily told her mother once. "Why doesn't a prince come and rescue you?"

Mama smiled. "Why, because I don't need a prince. I've got you, sweetie. We've got each other."

But sometimes Emily secretly thought it might be nice to have someone else around, too. Someone who'd ride her on his shoulders and tickle her feet, who'd bring her presents for no reason and teach her how to play baseball. Someone who'd come chase away the monsters from her closet and from underneath her bed before she fell asleep each night. Her friends had dads like that. Why couldn't she?

Emily stared up at the moon and wished for a dad, someone big and strong who would come and rescue her.

She blinked back tears because she knew that wishing wouldn't make it so. Even if she did have a dad, even if he did come and find her, how would he be able to rescue her through all those metal bars on the window?

Chapter Ten

A week later, a month after Emily had gone missing, Tess went back to work. The command post had officially shut down, although there were a handful of volunteers, along with Tess, who continued to work from a small back room in the community center whenever they could spare a few hours. The private detective she'd hired with Jared's money was still on the case, but so far, he'd turned up no new evidence, and the reward money had generated nothing but false leads.

As for Tess, returning to work was no longer an option. Bills were piling up, both at home and at work, and she'd lost clients as well as employees in her absence.

After her business had taken root two years ago, she'd rented a small office in downtown Eden with enough warehouse space in the back for supplies and equipment storage. Signing the lease on the space had been a big step because it signified the growth and evolution of a tiny enterprise that had been launched from Tess's kitchen table.

She'd started with one employee, herself, but in just six months' time, she'd been able to hire on help and had graduated from the trenches to spending most of her time negotiating contracts and courting new clients. She was proud of how far her business had come in such a short amount of time, but she also knew that if she didn't turn things back around very quickly, she'd find herself having to cut back the operation to the basics.

Well, she'd done it before and she could do it again if she had to, Tess thought with grim resolve. After all, opening a cleaning business in a town the size of Eden had seemed like folly to some.

But Tess had known from her mother's employment with the Spencers that the city people who owned vacation homes on the north side of Marvel Lake were willing to pay top dollar to someone they could trust to look after their sizable investments. They needed caretakers as well as housekeepers, someone who would keep an eye on their property during the week while they were away in the city, and who would see to repairs and upkeep in the winter when the homes were rarely used.

In the case of major repairs, like roof damage or plumbing, Tess would acquire bids from local contractors, submit them to her client, and once she was given the go-ahead, would then supervise the renovations from start to finish, thus alleviating the home owner of much of the headache.

And in addition to caring for the wealthy Sin City vacation homes, she'd also contracted the company's services to local businesses, including banks, office buildings and even Fairhaven Academy.

Before Emily's disappearance, Tess had twenty employees on her payroll, which meant ten crews working both day and evening shifts, and the business was starting to turn such a nice profit that she'd wanted to add another five crews, ten more employees. But that would have to wait now. The expansion would depend on whether or not she could reverse the company's fortunes, and how quickly.

On her first morning back, she set herself to that task, spending hours on the phone, apologizing to her clients and reassuring them that her services would be back up to speed in a reasonable length of time. She'd also managed to woo back the employees that had become discouraged or desperate during her long absence and had struck out on their own, just trying to get by.

By the time lunch rolled around, Tess was already exhausted, but she'd made substantial headway. And for the first time in weeks, she'd actually begun to feel useful again, like a productive member of society.

Putting aside the phone, she glanced at her watch, surprised at how quickly the morning had gone by. It was the first day since her daughter had been missing that time had actually seemed to fly for Tess. It was also the first time in days that she'd experienced hunger pains.

Ignoring the rumble in her stomach, she got up and walked over to the window to glance out. Emily's picture remained posted in store windows and on street signs, but a lot of them had blown away or been taken down. The yellow ribbons were disappearing, too, and in their absence came the children. Happy, innocent, they skipped along the street in their mothers' wake, oblivious to the darkness, to the shadow that still hung over the town.

But the shadow, too, was dissipating. In time, Tess's daughter would become nothing more than a sad memory to the residents of Eden. In time, everyone's lives would be completely back to normal. But Tess would never be the same. The hole in her heart would never completely heal.

She drew a hand across her eyes as she stared out into the brilliant, sunlit day.

"Tess?"

Jared's voice startled her, and she swung around to the door, her hand at her heart. She hadn't heard him come in, and the sight of him gave her a jolt. Her first thought when she saw him standing in the doorway was that he'd come to demand more answers. He'd come to force her into telling him the truth.

On the night they'd gone out looking for Emily together, Tess had seen something in his eyes, a revelation, as if it had suddenly occurred to him the real reason she'd left town six years ago. The real reason Emily had dark hair and dark eyes when Tess, herself, was so fair. Tess had thought to herself that night, *He knows. Deep down inside, he already knows. When that knowledge comes bubbling up to the surface, he's going to ask me point-blank if Emily is his daughter, and I'm not going to be able to lie to him. And then he'll go back and tell his family. Royce will find out...*

Tess had lived on pins and needles for days afterward, knowing that Jared could show up at any time and force a confrontation. But when the week ended and she'd had no word from him, she'd begun to relax. He didn't know about Emily. He couldn't.

But here he was now, and in spite of Tess's trepidation, a secret thrill raced through her. She couldn't deny the impact, the attraction. The connection that had built slowly between them on the night they'd gone out searching for Emily, and the even greater bond that had been forged six years ago. She couldn't deny that she still felt something for Jared Spencer, but there was danger in the temptation he offered her. If she let Jared back into her life, the serpent would be sure to follow.

He gave her a bemused look. "Why are you staring at me like that?"

She pushed a stray lock of hair behind her ear. "No reason. I'm just surprised to see you, that's all. How did you know where to find me?"

"I went out to the house, and when no one answered the door, I thought you may have come back to work. So I drove back into town and asked around."

He was dressed in an elegant gray suit that had undoubtedly been tailored to his broad shoulders and trim waist and hips. The color complimented his dark hair and eyes, and it hit Tess anew how extraordinarily handsome he was.

The years had added a maturity and strength to his features, and his accomplishments had given him confidence that, unlike the other Spencers, was still just shy of arrogance. He looked like a man comfortable in his own skin, Tess thought. A man who neither took for granted nor apologized for who he was or where he'd come from.

She waited for a twinge of the old resentment, but none came. Perhaps because she'd learned a week ago what she should have known and trusted six years ago. In spite of his heritage, or maybe even because of it, Jared Spencer had managed to remain a good and decent man.

He smiled at her now, as if he'd read her thoughts, and Tess's heart began to pound in earnest. She'd been cognizant of the attraction between them a week ago, but only peripherally. Her grief had obliterated all other emotions except fear, but now the attraction shot through her, and she felt almost breathless, almost stunned by its force.

She was a grown woman, for goodness' sake. She shouldn't be reacting so strongly to a good-looking man. But, of course, Jared wasn't just any man. He was an old lover. Her daughter's father, and that alone was an undeniable pull. That alone made him almost irresistibly sexy.

It was true, she thought in awe. The bond created by a child was like nothing else.

His expression still bemused, as if he couldn't quite figure her out, he glanced around the office. "When did you decide to come back to work?"

Tess walked over to her desk and sat down. "It wasn't so much a decision as a necessity. The bills were piling up…" She trailed off and shrugged. "Besides, it was time. I had to do this."

He nodded in understanding. "Have there been any developments?"

She gave him an ironic look. "You would know if there had been. Abby Cross said you stayed in constant contact. In fact, I get the distinct impression your calls have become something of a nuisance at the sheriff's station."

"I just want to make certain they're doing their job." He offered no apology for his interference.

At one time, his intervention, the Spencer influence, might have been grating, but Tess found that she didn't mind now. In fact, she welcomed it. If the Spencer connections could help bring Emily home, what did a little thing like pride matter?

"The reward has generated a lot of calls, but nothing has panned out so far," she told him.

"And the private investigator?"

"He interviewed me several days ago, and I know he's talked to the police on numerous occasions. But so far...nothing."

"I'm sorry, Tess."

She sighed, rubbing her hand across her forehead. "It's been a month. A month today."

"Is that why you chose today to come back to work?"

"I came back to work today because I had to." She riffled through a stack of bills on her desk. "I know it sounds trite, but life does go on. I have to work. I have people depending on me, obligations..." She glanced up at him. "And I have to find a way to pay you back."

A frown flitted across his features. "You don't need to worry about that."

"But I do. You loaned me a lot of money, Jared. The reward, the private investigator. I had no idea it would be so expensive."

"Money is the last thing you should have to worry about right now."

"That's easy for you to say," she said with a trace of the old bitterness.

His frown deepened as he gazed down at her. "Yes, it is easy for me to say. I have money. A lot of it. And I can use it to help you out if you'll let me."

"But why?" she asked helplessly.

His features hardened at her question. "There's no deep dark motivation on my part, if that's what concerns you. Having money doesn't automatically make me the villain."

"I know that."

"Do you?"

She lifted her shoulders. "Why do you even care what I think?"

He turned and walked over to the window to glance out. "I guess I've been asking myself that question for a long time now."

An awkward silence fell between them. After a moment, he turned from the window and came back over to her desk, placing his hands on the surface as he leaned toward her. "Look, Tess. I don't want to argue every time we're together. I don't want to talk about the past, either. For now, maybe we should just call a truce." He straightened, still gazing down at her. "We both want the same thing, after all. To find Emily and bring her back home."

Tess's eyes smarted with tears. "You must think me ungrateful after everything you've done. I'm not."

His gaze on her softened. "I know what you're going through. I know how hard things are for you right now, and it puts a lot of things into perspective for me, too. Maybe it's time we let bygones be bygones."

"You mean that?"

He gave her a wry smile. "I'm working on it." His gaze lingered on her for a moment, making Tess's heart beat even harder, and then he glanced away. He walked around the modest office. "So this is your company. Eden's Maid Brigade. I like the name."

"My friend Melanie came up with it. Although we're more than just a maid service," she offered tentatively.

"You've got a nice space here."

Tess glanced around, trying to see the office from his eyes. "It's a far cry from the corporate headquarters of the Spencer Hotels Corporation, but it serves my purpose."

Jared shrugged. "You're right. There's no comparison. I occupy an office I've been groomed for my whole life. You started your company from scratch. I have a board of directors that watches my every move, that pounces on my every mistake. You don't have to answer to anyone but your clients. If you want to expand, if you want to renovate, you don't have to file a dozen different prospectuses, and then try to sell your case to a group of stodgy old men who haven't had an innovative idea between them in thirty years. You've done this all on your own, and you should be proud.''

Tess blushed at his praise. ''Thanks, but I know how hard you've worked to get where you are.''

''Sometimes I wonder just where that is,'' he murmured. He glanced back at her. ''Tell me something, Tess. Why this particular line of work? I can't help wondering.''

She grew defensive again. ''There's nothing wrong with what I do. My mother cleaned up after your family for a lot of years, if you'll recall.''

''Yes,'' Jared said. ''And you always resented it.''

''Because she had no other choices. I do. I run this business on my own terms.''

He lifted one eyebrow. ''Meaning you like to stick it to the rich folks on the north side of the lake?''

Tess started to retort, but then she saw the hint of amusement in his eyes. She said grudgingly, ''I can see why you might think that, but the real reason I got into this business was because it was something I knew. I saw a need, and I filled it. I offer a valuable service at a fair price. There's nothing wrong with that.''

''Nothing at all. It's smart business,'' Jared agreed. ''You were always full of surprises.''

At the intimate tone in his voice, Tess cleared her throat. ''Yes, well, I'm sure you didn't drive all the way up here to discuss my business practices.''

"Actually, that's precisely why I'm here. I came to offer you a business proposition."

Tess glanced at him in surprise. "What kind of proposition?"

"I've bought back the lake house. The previous owners have already moved out, but I need someone to go in and clean the place up. I'm having furniture delivered on Thursday, and I can't be there, so I'll need someone present on that day to let the movers in."

"Wow," Tess said. "You don't waste time, do you?"

He shrugged. "Not when it's something I want, no. Actually, I closed on the place weeks ago."

Before she'd gone to see him? Tess wondered. But why? Why did he want a house in Eden these days?

"At any rate, I'd like to hire your company to whip the place into shape for me. Are you interested?"

She frowned. "I'm not sure that would be such a good idea."

"Why not? It's a straightforward business proposal, the kind we both negotiate every day. Why wouldn't it be a good idea?"

Tess supposed she should be flattered that he was putting her on an equal footing, businessman to businesswoman. But working with Jared, spending time with him—it just wasn't a good idea.

On the other hand, could she really afford to turn him down? After all, she owed him a great deal of money, and Tess didn't like to be indebted to anyone, especially someone who could potentially have as much power over her as Jared could. "I'll consider your proposition on one condition. The fee for my services will be applied against the money I owe you."

"Tess—"

She stood up, as if to emphasize her point. "That's the only way I'll agree. Otherwise, you'll have to find someone else."

"All right, agreed," he said in exasperation. He rose and held out his hand.

The moment his fingers closed over hers, Tess had an overwhelming feeling that her fate, along with their bargain, had just been sealed. "I'll draw up the contracts and have them sent to your office," she said nervously, slipping her hand from his.

He nodded. "Fair enough. How soon can you get started? I've promised my niece and nephew a trip to the lake as soon as possible."

"I'll go out there tomorrow and have a look around. Unless the place is a total wreck, I can probably have the cleaning done by the end of the week."

"Fair enough. One other thing." He pulled a credit card from the inner pocket of his jacket and plopped it on the desk. "I've opened up an account at Lawson's Department Store here in town. I've put your name on the account, too, so that you can purchase all the basics—linens, dishes, pots and pans. Whatever you think I'll need to start spending weekends at the house."

Tess stared down at the credit card for a moment, then glanced back up at him. "But I don't do that sort of thing. I'm not a personal shopper, much less a designer."

Jared shrugged again. "If I wanted a designer, I'd hire one. I don't. I want to keep things simple. I want the lake house to feel more like a home than a showplace. I want kids—my nephew and niece—to be able to run around inside, play and have a good time without worrying what they spill on the furniture. If they want to flop down on the sofa in wet swimsuits, then so be it.''

They must adore you, Tess thought. Aloud, she protested, ''You're asking too much of me. I can't turn your house into a home. I can't turn my whole schedule upside down just to accommodate you. If you don't want a designer, then why don't you just hire a personal shopper from Lawson's to do all this for you?''

''Because I trust you,'' he said softly. Then he gave her a challenging smile. ''Think of it this way. I'm offering you a chance to branch out. This could become a whole new service. Assuming, of course, that I'll be happy enough with your work to offer a recommendation.''

She snatched up the credit card from the desk and slipped it into her jeans pocket. ''I can assure you, you'll be quite pleased with my work. I've never once received a complaint. Now, if that's all—''

''Just one more thing.''

''Let me guess,'' Tess said dryly. ''You want me to weed the flower beds and cut the grass for you, too.''

Jared grinned. ''Actually, no. Nothing quite so physical. I'd like you to have lunch with me.''

Tess's heart gave an uncomfortable jolt. ''Uh, no, thank you. I have a lot of work to do. Especially now.''

''You have to eat sometime.''

''Then I'll just grab a sandwich and eat at my desk.''

''Come on, Tess. It's just a lunch between two people doing business together. Happens all the time.''

Yes, but they weren't just two people doing business. They were two people who shared a past, who shared a daughter, and the more time they spent together, the harder it would be for Tess to keep that secret.

THE LUNCH CROWD spilled out onto the sidewalk tables at the Paradise Café, but thankfully most of them seemed to be waiting for take-out orders. Tess and Jared made their way through the line at the cash register and found a table by the windows, where they could look out on the street.

After the harried waitress had taken their orders for club sandwiches and drinks, Tess said, "Don't expect too much. The food is good here, but it's hardly what you're used to."

Jared wondered if she would ever stop making comparisons between her life and his. "You know, Tess, I don't exactly lead the glamorous life you seem to think I do. In New Orleans, I stayed in a suite at the Spencer, and as nice as the accommodations are, living in a hotel leaves a lot to be desired. No neighbors. No friends. Most nights I ended up ordering room service for dinner. It's a pretty lonely existence."

"Then why didn't you get your own place?"

He shrugged. "I could have. But a home is more than just a place, and besides, it was easier to put in the kind of hours I needed to if I stayed on-site."

She toyed with her teaspoon. "If you were so busy, it's a wonder you had any time for a social life."

For some reason, Jared didn't think the comment was as innocent and casual as her offhand demeanor seemed to suggest. "Meaning?"

"Nothing." She lifted her chin, a gesture that was both familiar and endearing, even though it had often led to Jared's exasperation with her in the past. "I'm just surprised you had time for a serious relationship, that's all." When he didn't comment, she said, "So... how did you meet her?"

"Meet who?"

"Your fiancée."

"I told you the other day, I'm not engaged."

"Then why—" She stopped herself short and glanced down.

"Why did that article in the paper say otherwise?" he asked softly.

She glanced up and nodded.

"To tell you the truth, I don't know how it got in the paper, although I suspect my mother had something to do with it."

A frown flitted across Tess's forehead. "She did look like the type of woman your mother would approve of," she murmured. "Elegant. Sophisticated."

"My mother and I don't always share the same opinion," Jared said. "Nor do we have the same tastes."

"So who is she?" Tess persisted.

"Her name is Lauren Mathison."

"How did the two of you meet?"

"We met at the New Orleans Spencer."

"She was staying there?" Tess laid aside the teaspoon and picked up her fork, studying it as though it were the most interesting utensil in the world.

Watching her, Jared wondered about her sudden interest in his private life. Was it just curiosity or something more? He wanted it to be more, he suddenly realized. He wanted her to have that same punch-in-the-gut feeling he had every time he thought about her husband. About the two of them together. He turned that thought away quickly.

"She was working on a photo shoot in the lobby," he said almost curtly. "She's a model."

"A model?" Tess's expression looked almost crestfallen. She smoothed back her hair. "I guess the food

here in Eden may not be the only thing that doesn't
live up to your standards.''

"That's not true," he said softly. "You're still a
beautiful woman, Tess."

She glanced up, her hazel eyes meeting his before
glancing away. "I know what the last month has done
to me, both inside and out."

"Do you know what I see when I look at you, Tess?
I see a woman in great pain. A woman who loves her
daughter more than life itself." He reached over and
took her hand. "I see a woman who is still just as
beautiful as the day I caught her skinny-dipping in my
swimming pool."

To Jared's surprise, she didn't pull her hand away.
Instead, her fingers curled over his as her eyes shim-
mered with tears.

"WELL," Tess said a little while later. "Thank you for
lunch."

They were standing on the street in front of her office, and although the sidewalk was virtually deserted,
she had a feeling invisible eyes were watching them.
This was a small town, after all, and people liked to
talk. She could almost hear the gossip. *Look at that
Tess Campbell. Her little girl's only been missing a
month, and there she stands on the street corner, making eyes at some stranger.*

Of course, what they didn't know was that Jared was
hardly a stranger. He was Emily's father. He was the
only person in the world who could truly share in
Tess's grief, and it hit her suddenly just what her secret
had cost her. What it had cost Jared. He'd never gotten
to know his daughter, and now he might never get the
chance to.

As if sensing her turmoil, he put his hand under her chin and lifted her face to his. "It's going to be okay," he said. And then, before she had a chance to pull away, he bent and brushed his lips against hers.

"YOU WERE KISSING HIM! Right there on Main Street! The whole town probably saw you!"

Melanie's attack caught Tess completely off guard, and it took her a moment to respond. "I didn't kiss him. He kissed me."

"Oh, big difference!" Melanie snapped.

Tess had just come into the community center, and the two of them were alone. It was late, and Tess was exhausted. She'd worked until after six, organizing the night-shift assignments and the next day's schedule, and by the time she'd finally gotten to the center, Melanie was the only one there. She'd been sitting behind a computer terminal, apparently absorbed in her work, but the moment she'd glanced up, Tess had known something was wrong.

Melanie's face had an eerie, bluish cast in the light from the computer screen as she glared at Tess from across the room. Her eyes were almost electric. "How could you?"

Tess hardly knew what to say. She walked over and sat down beside Melanie. "It's not what you think."

"No?" Melanie turned off the computer screen and swung her wheelchair around to face Tess. "Then how is it? How was it you found yourself being kissed by Jared Spencer on Main Street, for the whole world to see, when you know as well as I do how dangerous he is?"

Tess pushed back her hair. "He's not dangerous, Melanie. I was never afraid of Jared."

"If you weren't afraid of him, then why didn't you go to him that night and tell him the truth about Royce? About the bracelet? About the baby?" Melanie demanded. "You may not have been afraid of him, but you sure as hell didn't trust him. And with good reason. He was, and always will be, a Spencer."

Tess glanced away, resisting the temptation to remind Melanie that she had begged Tess not to go to Jared that night. But Tess alone was responsible for her actions and her mistakes. She'd made her decision six years ago, and she'd had to live with it ever since. "Maybe I should have gone to him," she said in a quiet, regretful tone. "If I had, maybe things would be different. Maybe he could have found a way to stop Royce. Maybe he would have married me, and Emily would be safe and sound instead of—" She broke off, putting a hand to her mouth to control the sudden rush of emotion.

Melanie just stared at her. "Please tell me you aren't considering telling him the truth."

Tess glanced away. "Sometimes I think he may already know."

Melanie gasped. "About Emily? How could he know?"

Tess bit her lip. "It may be my imagination, but the other night when we were together, I sensed that he knew."

"The other night?" Melanie's gaze on her narrowed. "How often have you been seeing him?"

Tess lifted her chin, refusing to be put on the defensive. "He came by the night the police were there, when someone had been in the house. He stayed on for a while after they left because I didn't want to be alone."

"You could have called me or Joelle. Or Naomi. Why Jared?" Melanie asked sullenly. Her gaze on Tess grew accusing. "You're still in love with him, aren't you?"

Tess sighed. "I don't know if it's love. But we do have a connection. I can't deny that."

"Oh, God." Melanie shifted her chair away from Tess. "I was afraid this would happen."

"I just don't know what to do anymore," Tess said in confusion. "It was never fair to keep the truth from Jared. I knew that. But I did it because I was afraid of what Royce would do if he found out about the baby. But now, with Emily missing—"

Melanie whirled to face her. "How does that change anything?"

Tess shrugged helplessly. "He has a right to know."

"He had a right to know six years ago, but that didn't stop you from doing what you had to do to protect Emily. Look at me, Tess." Melanie's voice grew almost defiant, but there was also an underlying note of despair. "What do you think the last six years have been like for me? I always wanted to get married. I always wanted a family. What man would have me now?"

Tess's heart went out to her friend. "Oh, Melanie. You're still so beautiful. And you have so much to give. Any man would be lucky to have you."

"Lucky to have a woman who can't bear him children? There aren't many who would share your sentiment," she said bitterly.

"I wish things could have been different," Tess said softly. "Maybe if I could have gotten help faster that night…"

Melanie shook her head. "You did everything you

could do. I'm not blaming you. I've never blamed you. I'm glad you walked away. But—'' She reached over and took Tess's hand. ''Don't lose sight of why you left town. Why you never told Jared about Emily. Think back to that night, Tess. Remember how terrified you were. And with good reason. Royce Spencer would have killed you if he'd known about the baby. And there wouldn't have been anything Jared, or anyone else, could have done about it. You did the right thing.''

''God, I hope so.''

''You've always been the strongest person I know, Tess, but you can't let down your guard now. What if we find Emily? What if she comes back to us? Are you willing to take the chance that Jared can stop Royce from getting to her? That he'd even believe you over his own brother? Are you willing to risk your daughter's life to salvage your own conscience?''

Tess put her hands to her face. ''I just want her to come home.''

''I know you do,'' Melanie said soothingly. ''And that's why you aren't thinking clearly. But now is not the time to get careless. You still have to protect yourself.''

Melanie took both of Tess's hands in hers. ''You did the right thing by keeping silent. But if the truth comes out now, what do you think Royce would do? He'd be more dangerous than ever. And supposing Jared did believe you? What could either one of you prove? Nothing. Royce would get away scot-free, and then, in time, he'd come after you. He might even come after Jared, too. And neither one of you would see it coming.''

Tess felt as if a noose were slowly tightening around

her neck. She was still caught in Royce Spencer's trap. She was still bound by the same secret she'd sworn six years ago to take to her deathbed. And Jared? Nothing had changed between them. Not in all this time. They were still never meant to be.

"So Royce wins," she said angrily. "No matter what I do."

"At least you're alive," Melanie said harshly. "And as long as you're alive, you still have a chance to find Emily."

Chapter Eleven

By the time Jared's furniture arrived on Thursday, the lake house sparkled from all the polishing, scrubbing, and elbow grease Tess had applied to the task. She'd done most of the work herself because she couldn't afford to take any of her crews off her contracted jobs. She had a lot of goodwill to make up, although her customers had been very understanding about her absence. Still, she looked at Jared's contract as almost a side job, and it was her responsibility alone to fulfill it.

And, truth be known, maybe she was a little curious to see what he intended to do with the place. As she'd supervised the movers, she'd been struck immediately by the expensive but serviceable pieces of furniture he'd chosen. The sturdy leather sofa and chairs were in sharp contrast to the delicate white brocade fabrics that had adorned the house six years ago.

Evidently, he'd meant what he said. He wanted the lake house to be a place where kids could be kids, and Tess, perhaps for the first time, considered what his own childhood must have been like. She'd never been to the Spencer estate in Jackson, but, judging from the former grandeur of the lake house, she could well imagine the opulence, the stiff formality that would be the routine.

Tess had always resented the Spencers and their money, but now as she thought about the way Jared had grown up, the constant competitions, the impossible expectations, the sly manipulations, she realized that she was the lucky one. Her mother had allowed her at an early age to be her own person, to make her own decisions, and no matter what, Tess had known that she had Joelle's unconditional love. Tess had tried to raise Emily that way, too, but all the love in the world hadn't saved her from harm.

As Tess parked her truck in front of the lake house on Friday afternoon, she sat for a moment, reluctant to go inside. She wasn't sure why. It wasn't the tasks that still waited for her inside that made her hesitate. She'd never been afraid of hard work, and although she seldom went out on jobs herself these days, unless one of her crews was shorthanded, physical labor still didn't deter her.

But if it wasn't the work, then why did she get this uneasy feeling every time she came here? Why did she have the constant need to look over her shoulder, as if someone was watching her every move?

Tess had been to the house almost every afternoon this past week, so she knew there was nothing inside to be afraid of. So why the unease, the hesitation?

The hair at the back of her neck tingled as she gazed up at the windows, imagining someone inside, staring down at her.

"All right," she muttered, climbing out of the Explorer. "This is getting me nowhere fast."

Thunder rumbled in the distance, and she glanced worriedly toward the lake. Storm clouds gathered over the water, and Tess shivered, not keen on being caught on the wrong side of the lake in bad weather. It had been raining the night she and Melanie had had the accident. The night Tess had been fleeing from this very place in terror.

Don't think about that now, she warned herself sternly. She still had work to do inside, and if she didn't get started, she'd be here all night.

Using the key Jared had given her on Monday, she let herself into the house. It was only a little after three, but the coming storm made the house seem dark and gloomy in spite of all the windows. Tess quickly flipped on lights.

Better, she thought as she stood in the foyer glancing around. The house really was a masterpiece of design, with large, airy rooms leading into one another and floor-to-ceiling windows that provided breathtaking views of the lake, the pool and the gardens. She walked over to the wall of glass in the living room and stood for a moment, watching the storm bearing down over the water. An unexpectedly close clap of thunder sent her scurrying away from the windows.

"Okay," she muttered, gathering up the supplies she'd left earlier in the week. "Get busy and forget about the storm."

She paused at the bottom of the stairs, glancing around in satisfaction. The hardwood floors gleamed, the windows sparkled, and every nook and cranny had been scoured free of every speck of dust. Tess was nothing if not thorough, and she took a great deal of pride in her work. Not even a Spencer could find fault, she decided.

The place was still sparsely furnished. The leather furniture was scattered about the large living area, along with sturdy pine tables and armoires. But there were no accessories, no paintings on the walls, no lamps, no priceless objects of art. But somehow the room was more appealing than it had ever been before.

Tess remembered how it had looked on that fateful night six years ago, the sparkling chandeliers, the Chinese rugs, the white silk upholstery that had made her a nervous wreck as she'd moved about the room serving wine to the glitterati who'd come to celebrate the Spencers' anniversary. As if a glass of spilled wine was all she'd had to worry about, Tess thought dryly.

She shook her head, dispelling the memories, and hurried upstairs for one final inspection.

As she started down the hall, a noise somewhere in the house made her go stone still. Already jittery from the bad weather and from being alone, she felt a thrill of alarm go up her spine.

Nothing to be afraid of, she told herself firmly. Probably just thunder—

No, there it was again, and it was definitely not thunder. The sound was coming from somewhere down the hallway.

Tess's first thought was that perhaps someone had gotten inside the house, a homeless person seeking shelter from the coming storm. Or what if it was a convict hiding out from the law? Or Royce? What if he'd followed her out here?

What if her imagination ran completely away with her? Tess thought scornfully.

The noise, she decided, was nothing more than a tree branch scraping against the side of the house. Or, a tad more alarming, a mouse.

She walked down the hall, flipping on lights, but as she came to the end of the corridor, she paused, listening. Thunder rumbled outside, and she stood for a moment, rubbing her arms where electricity prickled along her skin.

This is crazy. There's no one here—
There!

The sound came from the third-floor attic. When Tess moved to the bottom of the steps, the rustling became more pronounced. Mice? she wondered again.

She climbed the steps slowly, telling herself there was nothing to be afraid of. No reason she shouldn't check out the attic and put her mind at ease once and for all so she could get on with her work.

The door to the attic was at the top of the stairs, and Tess remained poised on the top step, putting her ear to the wood. The rustling stopped, but after a moment another sound came to her. A very faint groan.

Her heart in her throat, Tess reached for the doorknob and turned it, but the door was locked. She rattled the knob uselessly as an impossible thought came to her. Could Emily be locked inside that room?

That's crazy! Tess told herself furiously. Emily had been missing for over a month. She couldn't have been locked up here in the lake house for all that time. She couldn't! It was impossible!

But what if she was?

Tess shook the knob frantically, then put a shoulder into the door and shoved. "Emily!"

Almost too late, she saw a shadow on the door that hadn't been there before. Someone had come up behind her in the hallway.

Whirling, Tess lost her balance and pitched forward down the stairs.

SHE CAUGHT HERSELF before she fell, and Jared came rushing up the steps toward her. "Tess? You okay?"

She sat down weakly on the stairs, massaging her right ankle. "Why did you sneak up on me like that?" she snapped. "You almost scared me to death!"

She looked pale as a ghost, Jared thought. He knelt in front of her. "I didn't mean to frighten you. I saw your truck out front, so I let myself in and came looking for you." He glanced down at her ankle. "Are you okay? Do I need to get you to a doctor?"

"No, I just twisted it." She stood, putting weight on the foot, and grimaced. "I'll live." She turned and glanced back up the stairs. "I was trying to get in the attic. The door's locked. Do you know why?"

Jared rose, too, and walked past her up the stairs, trying the door for himself. "I don't think it's locked. I think it's just stuck." He put a shoulder against the wood, and, after a split second, the hinges squealed ominously. He shoved the door open and reached inside to turn on the light.

Tess came up behind him. "What's in there?"

"Junk mostly, left behind by the previous owners, I'd guess." He stepped back. "Want to see for yourself?"

She moved in front of him, walking through the door as her gaze swung around the cluttered space.

"Why did you want to get in the attic?" Jared asked her.

She glanced back at him, her expression guarded. "I thought I heard something. I think you may have mice."

"Then why were you calling for Emily?"

In the stark light from the bare bulb suspended from

the ceiling, he saw her flinch. But she said nothing as she moved around the room, searching.

"Tess?"

She gave him a guilty look. "My imagination got the better of me, okay? I thought I heard a…cry or a groan. It sounded like a child."

No sooner were the words out of her mouth than Jared heard the noise, too.

Tess's face went even paler, and she glanced frantically around the attic. "Did you hear that?"

He strode by her to the window. "There's your culprit." He nodded toward the window. When Tess came to stand beside him, he pointed outside. A weather vane on the roof turned in the wind. The metal moaned as it twisted, sounding a little like a child in distress.

"That's all it was. Nothing to be alarmed about."

Tess wrapped her arms around her middle and glanced around. "I guess you're right."

"Shall we go?"

She nodded and followed him out. He closed the attic door and the two of them descended the steps together. At the bottom, he paused and took Tess's arm. "Are you sure you're okay?"

"I told you. I just twisted my ankle. It'll be fine—"

"I'm not talking about your ankle. Tess." He gazed down at her, searching her face. "Why would you think Emily would be up in that attic?"

"I didn't. I mean…not really. But I hear her all the time, calling out to me. I see her everywhere." Her eyes filled with tears and she turned away. "Every house I drive by, every building I pass, I can't help wondering if she's inside. I know it sounds crazy, but I have the strongest feeling, even after all this time, that she's somewhere close by."

Not crazy so much as wishful thinking. But Jared understood. He caught himself thinking the same thing at times. If he could just search through every house in Eden, he'd be able to find her.

"Let's get you downstairs and have a closer look at that ankle."

"I told you, I'm fine—"

But a clap of thunder caused her to jump. The lights flickered and went out. In the murky light from the window, Jared saw her shudder.

He put his arm around her shoulders. "Nothing's changed up here at the lake, I see. We always used to lose power even in the mildest storms."

"There're some candles in the kitchen," Tess said. "I put them there myself."

Downstairs, Jared insisted that she sit while he retrieved the candles from the kitchen and got them going in the living room. Tess watched as he placed them around the room. In the flickering light, his features looked dark and mysterious. She shivered, thinking about what she'd told Melanie on Monday. *"I was never afraid of Jared."*

It was true. He'd never been a threat to her physically, but there was danger here just the same. Danger in the memories. In the emotions. In the attraction.

Danger in being trapped in a storm with the only man she'd ever been in love with.

Danger in the desire that was stronger than ever to tell him the truth about their daughter.

But more of her conversation with Melanie came back to her. *"Don't lose sight of why you left town,"* she'd warned. *"Why you never told Jared about Emily. Think back to that night, Tess. Remember how terrified you were. And with good reason. Royce Spencer would have killed you if he'd known about the baby. And there wouldn't have been anything Jared, or anyone else, could have done about it. You did the right thing."*

Then why did she feel as if she was being torn in two different directions? Tess wondered. If she'd done the right thing, why had guilt eaten away at her all these years? Guilt for keeping Emily from Jared. Guilt for walking away from an accident that had trapped Melanie in a wheelchair. Guilt that she should have been able to do something, *anything,* to stop Royce Spencer from ruining all their lives.

And she was still letting her fear of Royce control her. Maybe it was past time for the truth to come out. Maybe it was high time Royce Spencer be made to pay for what he'd done all those years ago.

"...if the truth comes out now, what do you think Royce would do? He'd be more dangerous than ever. And supposing Jared did believe you? What could either one of you prove? Nothing. Royce would get away scot-free, and then, in time, he'd come after you. He might even come after Jared, too. And neither one of you would see it coming."

Her thoughts in turmoil, Tess got up and limped over to the window. The storm was a mild one. It would pass quickly, leaving no damage other than fallen leaves and bruised flowers. Power would be restored and everything would return to normal.

Tess wished she could take comfort in that knowledge, but the tempest inside her would never be over. Not until Emily was back home, safe and sound. Not until Jared was out of her life, once and for all. Or until she told him the truth. Because she couldn't have it both ways, Tess realized. She could not continue to see Jared and keep her secret. It would destroy her.

And when he found out? She shuddered to think of that time.

He came up behind her and put his hands on her shoulders. Tess knew that she should move away, but instead, she found herself relaxing against him, drawing comfort from his touch, drawing courage from his strength.

"Why did you come out here alone?" he asked her.

She turned in surprise. "We had a deal, remember? I faxed you the contracts."

He frowned down at her. "Yes, but I didn't expect you to do the actual work yourself. I thought you'd send one of your crews. I only meant for you to organize."

Tess shrugged. "My crews are all busy. I can't afford to short-change my regular clients any more than I already have. There was no one left to do the work but me, and besides, I don't mind."

"Why do I have a feeling there's more to it than that?" Jared mused.

Tess frowned. "I don't know what you mean. It's purely a matter of management and economics."

"Nothing to do with pride?"

"Pride?" She stared up at him blankly.

"A way to put us both back in our places? A way to remind me, yet again, that we were never meant to be?"

Tess's heart thudded against her chest. "The thought never even occurred to me."

"Then maybe there's hope after all," he murmured. His gaze on her deepened, and Tess knew what was coming. He was going to kiss her, and she was going to let him because she was powerless to stop it.

No, that's not true, a little voice whispered. *You don't want to stop it.*

No man had kissed her since Jared. No man had held her since Jared. Her relationship with Alan had been nothing more than a tender friendship, two needy people trying desperately to chase away the loneliness. There'd been love, but no romance. Touching, but no passion. Tess had told herself that she didn't miss a physical relationship with a man. In some ways, holding hands with Alan had been just as fulfilling, especially toward the end, but staring up at Jared now, she realized how badly she'd been deluding herself.

Making love with him had been like sharing a piece of heaven. The two of them alone on his boat, the night wind cooling their feverish bodies as they moved in perfect sync, their souls melding…

Together, they'd found paradise, and they'd made Emily under a deep velvet sky filled with stars.

He thumbed away tears Tess hadn't even realized were falling. And then he lowered his mouth to hers.

It was a gentle kiss, warm and experimental, with just a hint of urgency. With just a whisper of the old passion, as if he was holding off, waiting for her reaction. Now was the time to back off, Tess told herself. Now was the time to pull away. But she didn't. Instead, she opened her lips, tentatively touching her tongue to his.

She felt a shudder go through Jared's body as his arms wrapped around her and he drew her close, kissing her deeply as his mouth moved against hers, as his tongue met hers in a breathtaking dance of desire.

Tingles skimmed along her spine as she wound her

arms around his neck. They were standing so close she could feel his heartbeat against her own. The wild rhythm was like a synergist, a chemical reactor that stoked her memories, that fueled images of the way things had been with Jared, of the way things would still be if they gave in to their wildest yearnings.

He broke the kiss, burying his face in her hair. "Tess, Tess. Do you have any idea how much I want you? How much I need you?"

She closed her eyes as the power of his words swept over her. "I want you, too," she whispered.

He tunneled his fingers through her hair, holding her back a little so that he could gaze into her eyes. "Do you have any idea how long I've waited to hear you say that?"

"Yes. I do know. I do."

"Why did you leave me?" He pulled her back to him, smoothing his hand down her hair. "No, don't answer that. It doesn't matter."

But it did. Because the threat that had driven her from him that night still existed. And if she let him back into her life, he could be in danger, too.

She drew away from him. "I should go."

"Why?" He stared down into her face.

"Because if I stay here…"

When she trailed off, Jared said, "You might lose control? Would that be so terrible?"

"Yes, it would." She took a step back from him, putting a physical distance between them. "I can't do this, Jared. I can't…let myself lose control. Not while Emily is still out there somewhere. I can't."

She turned frantically toward the door, but then stopped in her tracks when the doorbell sounded. She stared at the foyer. If that was Royce—

"Who could that be?" Jared muttered, walking past her to the door. He glanced out the window, then turned back to Tess, his expression grave. "It's Abby Cross."

Tess's hand flew to her throat. "Oh, no. Emily—"

She shot by Jared and grabbed for the door, but he was already drawing it back. Abby's expression seemed to say it all. She looked grim.

Tess swayed, grabbing the edge of the door for support. "No. Please, no." Jared put his arm around her, and Tess didn't resist. She didn't have the strength.

"It's not what you think," Abby said quickly. Rain dripped from her dark hair as her gaze went from Tess to Jared. If she wondered why the two of them were alone out here, she didn't ask. "Your mother told me I could find you here. We don't know anything for certain yet, but I wanted to tell you myself before you heard anything on the news."

"What?" Tess said in anguish. "Just tell me."

"The body of a child was found in Grover County—"

A loud roaring filled Tess's ears, and as if from a distance, she heard Abby say, "We don't think it's Emily, Tess. In fact, we know it's not—"

But it was too late. Tess sagged against Jared, and his arm was the only thing that kept her from falling to the floor.

Chapter Twelve

"Tess, you didn't need to come down here. We'll let you know as soon as we hear anything." Sheriff Money sat back in his chair and regarded her with a sympathetic smile across the expanse of his desk.

"Abby said you were expecting a phone call from the sheriff down in Grover County with some more information. I wanted to be here when you got the call." Tess was still trembling. She hadn't been able to stop shaking since she'd seen Abby Cross outside Jared's door. The fact that Abby had told her over and over that they didn't think the remains were Emily hadn't helped. All Tess could think about was her little girl—

As if sensing her emotions, Jared, standing behind her, rested his hands on her shoulders. His presence was more reassuring than Tess should allow it to be.

Abby had accompanied them to the sheriff's station, and she paced the office now, her gaze occasionally meeting Tess's. A terrible understanding passed between them.

"I just put another call in to him," Sheriff Mooney said. "His secretary said he'd get right back to me."

No sooner had the words left his mouth than the

phone rang, and Sheriff Mooney snatched it up. He listened for a moment, then said, "Yeah, put him on, Doreen." A pause. "This is Sheriff Mooney. You got some information for me, Don?"

The silence that followed was punctuated occasionally by "I see" and "I understand" and finally, before he ended the call, "Well, good luck to you. Tough business we're in," he said grimly. Hanging up the phone, he glanced up. "That was Sheriff Don Webber."

Tess tried to brace herself as she searched Sheriff Mooney's face for some sign, some clue that would allay her worst nightmare. "What did he say?"

"Here's what he knows so far. Two days ago, a body was recovered in a densely wooden area in Grover County, which is down near the Louisiana border. It looks to be that of a child, but the remains are badly decomposed. In fact, there's little more than bones to go on. They called in Dr. Barbara Wesley, a forensic anthropologist from the forensics lab at LSU, to help in the excavation and identification. Tess—" he leaned forward, his gaze meeting hers "—according to Dr. Wesley's preliminary findings, there's no way it can be Emily."

Relief surged like a shot of pure adrenaline through Tess's bloodstream. Jared's grasp on her shoulders tightened, and without thinking, she put one of her hands up to his. "Are they sure?"

Sheriff Mooney's expression remained austere, as if talking about the death of a child, any child, took something out of him. "Like I said, the remains were badly decomposed. The body's been there for a while. Dr. Wesley says anywhere from five to ten years."

A gasp sounded from behind her, and Tess glanced

around. Naomi Cross stood in the doorway of the sheriff's office, her hand at her heart, her face a ghastly white.

"Sadie," she said on a whisper.

"POOR NAOMI," Tess murmured as she and Jared left the sheriff's station. "I feel so badly for her. She's helped me so much since Emily's disappearance. I wish there was something I could do for her."

Jared opened the car door for Tess, and then he went around and got behind the wheel.

"I know you feel badly for Naomi, but they don't know that the remains are Sadie's. It'll take the forensic anthropologist several days at least to make a final determination. If she ever can."

Tess shuddered. "I know. All I could think about in there was thank God it wasn't Emily. Thank God she could still be alive. And then I saw Naomi's face. I saw that terrible look in her eyes, and I knew what she was going through. It doesn't get any easier. Not in a year or five years or even ten. You never give up the hope that your child might still be found alive."

Tess turned to stare out the window, but Jared knew she wasn't watching the passing scenery. She was seeing herself in Naomi Cross's eyes. She was seeing herself ten years from now.

The death of a child was a horrible thing, something a parent would never get over, Jared thought. But a missing child left a vacuum, an emptiness that could never be resolved, that could never be accepted. A missing child was like a great gaping wound that never completely healed. It might get better in time, but the slightest stress could rip it open without warning.

"I'll drive you home," he said to Tess. "You can pick up the Explorer tomorrow."

"No." She turned to face him. "I don't want to go home. I can't be there right now." She rubbed her arms with her hands. "I can't be there without her."

"We'll go back to the lake house then."

Tess said nothing. She turned back to the window, searching the landscape, Jared thought, for some sign, some hope that Emily was still alive.

But once they got to the house, she stood just inside the door, as if she didn't have a clue how she'd gotten there.

"You're trembling," Jared murmured. "You need to get out of those wet clothes."

"I'm okay," she protested.

"It's been a rough day," he said softly. "Let me take care of you."

She nodded almost absently, and Jared took her hand, leading her through the master bedroom into the bathroom. Reaching inside the massive shower stall, he turned on the water. Within seconds, the room grew steamy.

He started toward the door. "I'll give you some privacy—"

She caught his arm. "No, don't leave me." When he hesitated she hugged her arms tightly around her. "I don't want to be alone, Jared. I keep thinking about Naomi. I keeping think how I would feel if I thought Emily…if it was her…" She trailed off, shivering violently. "Would you just hold me?"

Jared pulled her into his arms and held her tightly. He smoothed his hand down her hair. "It'll be all right, Tess. It will."

"I'm so scared, Jared. I feel so alone."

"Shush. You're not alone. I'm here."

"Just hold me," she whispered raggedly. "Don't let me go."

"I won't. Ever." He plowed his fingers through her hair, lifting her face to his. She tilted her head back, and as her eyes fluttered closed, Jared brushed his lips against hers. It was meant to be a gentle kiss, a soothing kiss, but her lips parted, and the desperation and fear of the last few hours took over.

Jared deepened the kiss, groaning softly as she responded, as she wound her arms around his neck and pulled him to her.

"Please, please," she murmured when Jared broke the kiss. Her fingers were on the buttons of his shirt, and he shrugged out of it, tossing it into a corner. The rest of their clothes followed in kind, and then they were back in each other's arms, drawing comfort from the warmth of their bodies, losing themselves in the oblivion of passion.

If she was using him to forget, Jared understood. He didn't care. Maybe they were using each other. Maybe they were the only two people in the world who could understand what the other was feeling at that moment.

They moved into the shower and stood under the piercing cascade. The water was hot, bracing, healing. Jared stood behind her, running his hands down her arms, her waist, her hips. She arched against him, reaching up to cup the back of his neck and pull him toward her for a long, breathtaking kiss.

Her skin felt warm and sensuous beneath the water, her lips demanding and needy, and yet, somehow, innocent. Jared remembered the first time they'd been together, her innocence then, and her shy anticipation, her willingness to trust him in the most intimate way a woman could trust a man. He wanted that same trust now. He wanted to take care of her always. He wanted to never let her down.

She'd stocked the bathroom with expensive shampoos and French-milled soap from Lawson's Department Store, and Jared lathered his hands, smoothing them over her, touching her everywhere until she trembled beneath the water and turned in his arms.

He lifted her, kissing her long and deep while their bodies, at long last, became one again.

"YOU'RE AWFULLY QUIET."

They were in Jared's bed, nestled against the soft Egyptian cotton sheets Tess had also purchased for him at Lawson's. She lay on her back, gazing at the ceiling.

"Tess?"

She turned her head on the pillow and gazed at him. He lay on his side, propped on his elbow, bare to his waist where the sheet didn't cover him.

Her stomach quivered with awareness, and she glanced away.

"Are you giving me the silent treatment because you're upset?" he asked softly, but there was an edge to his voice that Tess couldn't quite define.

She shook her head on the pillow. "I don't mean to be giving you the silent treatment. I just don't know what to say. But I'm not upset."

"Having regrets?"

Her voice softened. "No. I needed that to happen. I needed…to be held. Thank you for being there for me."

He smiled. "My pleasure."

He said it in a way that made Tess blush. "I feel a little strange," she admitted.

"Strange how?"

"Like all this—" she lifted a hand, then let it fall back to the bed "—isn't quite real."

"Like we've gone back in time?"

She turned to face him. "Yes, exactly. Do you feel it, too?"

"I feel as if I've just been marking time for the last six years."

"Jared—"

"Don't say it, Tess." He lifted her hand to his lips. "Don't say it was a mistake. Don't say it can't happen again. Don't say it's over."

Her eyes filled with tears at his tenderness. "There's so much about me you don't know. Things I've kept...hidden."

His gaze on her deepened. "It's time for the truth to come out, Tess. You know that, don't you?"

She opened her mouth to protest, but he placed a fingertip over her lips. "But for now, all I want to do is hold you in my arms."

JARED WAS GONE when Tess awakened. It was dark in the bedroom except for a thin sliver of light from the bathroom. Tess sat up, pulling the sheet around her as she glanced at her watch in the light. It was only a little after nine. Still early, but her mother might be worried if she'd tried to reach Tess at home or at work.

The phone service hadn't yet been turned on at the lake house, and Tess wasn't sure where she'd left her cell phone. She climbed out of bed and went in search of her clothes. Jared had hung them up at some point, and even though they were still a little damp, Tess pulled them on, struggling a little with the jeans.

She went out into the hallway, crossed the foyer, and

walked into the living room. Light shone from beneath the kitchen door, and Tess smelled coffee. She opened the door and glanced inside. The kitchen, with its glass-fronted cabinets, hardwood floors and stainless-steel appliances gleamed from her efforts. With the aroma of freshly brewed coffee wafting on the air, the room seemed almost homey, a quality she would never have ascribed to it six years ago.

Jared's briefcase lay open on the table, and he'd left a stack of papers and a cup of coffee nearby. He couldn't have been gone long. The coffee still steamed.

A prickle of alarm stole up Tess's spine as she walked over to the table. The top sheet looked to be a report Jared had generated regarding proposed expansion to the Biloxi Spencer.

She left the papers where she'd found them, and looked around uneasily. "Jared?"

Her gaze moved back to the papers, to the cup of coffee. He'd obviously been working. What had drawn him away so quickly?

She glanced at the open briefcase. More papers inside. A stack of folders. The top one with her name on it.

Tess froze.

Why would Jared have a folder in his briefcase with her name on it?

Taking another quick perusal of the room, she lifted the file from the briefcase and opened it.

The first page was a letter from the same private-detective firm Tess had hired to search for Emily. Scanning the contents, she grew even more agitated. She sat down at the table and read the letter carefully. Jared had hired the firm to probe into her background. They'd been to Memphis, talked to people she'd gone to college with, interviewed nurses and doctors at the hospital where Alan had worked and where Tess had given birth to Emily.

Pausing for a moment in her reading, Tess thumbed through the documents attached to the letter. A copy of Emily's birth certificate. A copy of Alan's death certificate. Notes from the many interviews the investigator had conducted with Tess's acquaintances, including Alan's mother, who admitted she'd been opposed to her son's marriage to Tess. Who categorically denied that Emily was her grandchild. A notation on the side confirmed Alan's AIDS-related death.

Her heart pounding, Tess turned back to the letter.

It is our conclusion, based on numerous interviews conducted with Alan Campbell's friends, relatives and business associates, that he did not, in fact, father the aforementioned child. Also, according to at least two witnesses who worked at the hospital at the time Tess Campbell was admitted, the month she gave birth was April, not August. It is our opinion that hospital records were altered some time after Mrs. Campbell's baby was born and should you wish us to continue, we'll pursue evidence to that end.

However, we believe we've garnered sufficient information and testimony at this time to petition the court for a paternity test should you want to seek custody. Please advise if you wish us to continue. Yours truly…

Tess's hands were shaking by the time she finished the letter. Jared knew about Emily. He *knew*. But for how long? The letter was dated a week ago. Why hadn't he said anything?

Quickly, Tess paged through the report, searching for some clue as to why Jared might have kept silent. There were several other documents inside the folder, and Tess riffled through them too. Near the bottom was a blue-backed legal document that she recognized immediately as a copy of Davis Spencer's will, along with another lengthy document that explained the terms of the trust. The trust that awarded fifty million dollars to the first Spencer grandchild. The legal terms and fine print all blurred before Tess's eyes, and she felt almost sick with what she'd just learned, with her suspicions.

Jared wanted that money for himself.

That was why he'd been so eager to come back into Tess's life, why he'd been so willing to help her find Emily. He didn't care about Tess. He didn't care about Emily. All he wanted was the money. All he wanted was to win.

The back door opened and Jared stepped inside. He was dressed in jeans and a cotton pullover shirt. And he was barefoot. He didn't look like a man capable of such a deception at that moment. He didn't even look like a Spencer. But appearances were deceiving. According to what Tess had just read, he was as ruthless and single-minded as the rest of his family. Tess had been a fool for ever thinking he was different.

He glanced at her in surprise. "I thought you were sleeping."

She said nothing.

"Damnedest thing," he said, scratching his head. "I heard a car pull up outside. But when I went out to investigate, it pulled away."

Tess remained silent, and Jared frowned. "Are you

okay?" Then his gaze dropped to the open folder in her hands. He closed his eyes briefly.

"How long have you known?" she asked coldly.

"Let me explain—"

"How long?" she all but screamed.

Surprise flickered across his face at her outburst. "A few days."

She got up and faced him, anger rolling through her like a tidal wave. "Why, Jared? For God's sake, why didn't you tell me you knew?"

He lifted his gaze to hers, and his eyes seemed to darken with emotion, with his own anger. "Why didn't *you* tell *me*? Why did I have to hire a private investigator to find out I have a daughter? You knew when you left here six years ago that you were pregnant. Why didn't you tell me?"

"Because I didn't find out for sure until I was in Memphis, and by then it was too late. You'd wasted no time in moving to New Orleans."

"Oh, and you couldn't have called me? You couldn't have come to see me? Give me a break, Tess."

She lifted her chin defiantly. "I made a deal with your father. I promised—"

"To hell with my father," he raged, then turned away, rubbing the back of his neck as if that would somehow help him regain a grip on his temper. He turned back to Tess, his expression almost rigid with the effort of his control. "Why didn't you tell me?" he asked again.

"I didn't want to go to jail—"

The control slipped. "Stop it, Tess. Just stop it. You're still not telling me the truth."

"And neither are you." She glanced around the

kitchen. "You didn't buy this place back so you could play the doting uncle. You bought it for Emily. When I find her, you plan to try to take her away from me, don't you? But I warn you, Jared. I'll fight you," she said through gritted teeth. "I'll fight you with everything I've got."

He looked at her as if she were a stranger to him. The anger seemed to melt away, and all that was left was a look of almost unbearable sadness. "I never wanted to take her away from you. I just wanted you to tell me the truth."

He walked across the room toward her, but Tess took a step back from him. Jared stared at her for the longest moment, then he said quietly, "For once in your life, why can't you just trust me?"

"This is why." Her hands trembled as she held up the folder. "It's all about winning to you. It's all about beating Royce out of your father's trust."

"That's a low blow, Tess. I want to find Emily as much as you do. I'd give anything to be able to bring her home safe and sound." His gaze on her hardened. "And while we're throwing around accusations—how did you find out about my father's trust?"

"It's all in here." She held up the folder again.

But Jared shook his head. "No, you knew about it before. I can see it in your face. How did you find out?"

"It doesn't matter how I found out," Tess said coldly. "What matters to me is the lengths you were willing to go to to get what you wanted. You had me investigated, Jared. You violated my privacy. How do you think that makes me feel?"

"Betrayed?" he shot back. "I know exactly how you feel."

"Did you know about Emily when I came to see you at your office that day?" she asked him.

"No, not exactly. The day before you came, my secretary showed me a picture of Emily in the paper. I felt something. I don't know how to explain it. It was like…a connection. I couldn't stop looking at her picture. And then you came to see me the next day. You told me she was your daughter. I thought at first that explained why I was so drawn to her. Then I started thinking about it. Started wondering why she resembled me more than you. Not so much in looks. She's the spitting image of you in a lot of ways…" He trailed off, his gaze, it seemed to Tess, softening as he glanced at her. "But she has my coloring. My eyes. She's my daughter, isn't she, Tess?"

"You already know that."

"But I want to hear you say it. I want to hear you tell me what you should have told me a long time ago. Emily is my daughter."

"Yes," Tess whispered.

He pulled out a chair and sat down heavily at the table. "She's my daughter, and I've never even seen her. I never got to hold her when she was a baby. I never got to rock her. To see her take her first step. Hear her say her first word. I missed out on so much, and now…" He closed his eyes. "What if it's too late?"

Her own anger melting away, Tess crossed the floor and knelt beside him. "I'm sorry, Jared. I didn't want it to be this way. I didn't. But I didn't think I had any other choice."

"Why?"

She drew a long, steadying breath. "Because if I'd stayed, I was afraid Royce would kill me."

She told him everything then. About Melanie showing up at her house in hysterics the night Royce had threatened her. About Tess's mother warning her to stay away from the Spencers, including Jared. About her confrontation with Cressida the night of the party, and how Tess had known that she would never be accepted by the Spencers. She told him about overhearing Royce and Ariel, about Royce's plan to set her up for stealing his mother's bracelet, about his willingness to do whatever it took to gain control of that trust.

She told him about how panic had caused her to flee that night. How she'd wanted to run to him, but she'd been too afraid.

And she told him about the accident, about seeing Melanie trapped in the wreckage, her plea to never let Royce find out about the baby.

When she finished, she glanced up. Jared's face was ravaged with emotion. "If you'd come to me, I would have protected you. I would have killed him, my own brother, before I would have let him hurt you. Or Emily. You could have trusted me. But the fact that you didn't, that you still don't—" He glanced at the folder in her hands. "What hope has there ever been for us? You condemned me a long time ago because of who I am."

The truth of his words were like a nail driven into her heart. "I'm sorry, Jared. I'm so sorry. I didn't want it to be this way. If it had just been me, I would have come to you. But I couldn't take a chance with my baby—"

"You said you didn't even know you were pregnant when you left town."

"I didn't know for sure, but I suspected. And I couldn't take a chance. I didn't know what Royce would do. All I knew was that he was dangerous. And if I'd come forward with what I knew, if I'd told you the truth, I was afraid that Royce would somehow find a way to turn you against me.''

''Then you didn't know me very well,'' Jared said grimly. ''If you thought I would have ever taken his word over yours, if I would have ever chosen my family over you—''

''I *didn't* know. I couldn't take that chance,'' Tess said desperately. ''Can't you understand that?''

''Oh, I understand,'' Jared said quietly. ''And if you keep saying those words long enough, maybe one of these days you might actually start to believe them.''

He got up and walked toward the door.

Tess rose. ''Where are you going?''

''To find Royce.''

The look in his eyes made Tess's blood go cold. She grabbed his arm. ''Jared, don't. Please. Not until you've calmed down.''

''I'm calm, Tess. I've never been so calm. And I know exactly what I have to do.'' He glanced down at her hand on his arm, then back up. ''Let go.''

''You can't do this,'' she pleaded.

''You made your decision six years ago,'' he said without emotion. ''Now I've made mine.''

Chapter Thirteen

By the time Tess arrived home, she was emotionally and physically exhausted. Jared had gone to find Royce, and she didn't know what to do. She didn't know where to find him, how to stop him. She didn't even know what he planned to do.

I should never have told him. I should have listened to Melanie and kept silent.

Except that silence was no longer an option. Jared had found out about Emily on his own. With the help of a private detective, he'd put enough together to have very strong suspicions. Enough to take Tess to court to try to win custody.

Would he really do that?

She didn't want to believe that Jared would hurt her that way, but deep down inside, a part of her couldn't blame him. How would she feel if Emily had been kept from her all these years? How would she feel to find out, finally, that she had a daughter, when it might be too late to hold her, to love her, to watch her grow up?

She would feel just as Jared did—angry, hurt, betrayed. She'd want to lash out at someone, just as he did. But Royce Spencer was a very dangerous man. If

Jared confronted him, threatened him, there was no telling what he might do.

Tess let herself into the house and turned on lights as she walked out into the kitchen. She stared at the phone for a moment, wondering if she should call Cressida Spencer. Or Ariel. But what if that only served to warn Royce? What if he would be lying in wait when Jared found him?

Tess hovered over the phone, and when it rang she jumped as if it were gunfire. She grabbed up the receiver. "Jared?"

A pause. "No, I...Tess? It's Willa Banks."

"Hello, Miss Willa."

"Are you all right? You sound upset."

Tess massaged her forehead with her fingertips. "It's just been a long day."

"I understand. You're upset about that little girl's body that was found down south, aren't you?"

"How did you know about that?" Tess asked in surprise. "Has it already been on the news?"

"I was at the sheriff's station when you came in. And I saw Naomi leave. She looked so distraught. That poor child—" Willa's voice broke. "It's not right, all the suffering she's been through. It's not right."

"I know."

"She had another child, you know. There were two babies. I worked at the hospital back then. I was there that night. So many people died in that awful storm. There was so much confusion."

"It was terrible," Tess murmured, wanting desperately to get off the phone.

"It's not right that she lost both of them. When Sadie disappeared, I couldn't believe it. I couldn't understand it. How could both of her babies be taken away from her?''

"Miss Willa, I'm sure Naomi appreciates your concern."

"She's such a dear person," Willa said. "So deserving."

"Yes, I know." Tess hesitated. "Was there a reason for your call, Miss Willa?"

"I'm sorry for rambling on like that. I just get so upset sometimes."

"I understand."

"I wanted to let you know that I came by a little while ago with a batch of brownies for you. You weren't home so I left them on the back porch. I thought I'd better call you before some animal got into them."

"Thank you, Miss Willa, but you really shouldn't have gone to the trouble."

"Oh, it was no trouble at all. I love to bake. I made those especially for you. Double fudge, no walnuts. Just the way you like them."

Tess frowned at the phone. How did Miss Willa know about her favorite brownie recipe?

"Well, I'll let you go. You try to get a good night's rest," Willa said. "And don't forget about those brownies."

"I won't. And thanks again." Tess hung up and walked over to the back door, opening it to peer outside. The box of brownies had been placed on a lawn chair, and when Tess picked them up, the container was still warm. She must have just missed Willa.

She brought the box back into the kitchen and sat it on the counter. It was after ten o'clock at night. Willa lived all the way over on the other side of Mount Ida, near the lake. Why would she have driven all that way at this time of night to deliver a box of brownies?

"Double fudge, no walnuts. Just the way you like them."

"Oatmeal raisin. They're your favorite, aren't they?"

Tess's heart started to pound as she gazed at the box. How did Willa Banks know that oatmeal raisin cookies were her favorite? How did she know that Tess preferred brownies without walnuts?

Oatmeal raisin cookies were Emily's favorite, too. She didn't like nuts in brownies, either.

Tess put her hand to her mouth as something Melanie said came back to her. *"…she's not playing with a full deck, Tess. I don't think she should be allowed anywhere near those children…"*

A terrible suspicion, a horrible fear rose inside Tess, and she felt weak, sick. She reached for the phone.

After five rings, Melanie finally picked up. "Hello?" She sounded breathless, impatient.

"Melanie, it's me. Do you really think Willa Banks could be dangerous?" Tess said in a rush.

"What?"

Tess took a deep breath, trying to calm herself. "You said you didn't think she should be allowed near the children. Do you think she's dangerous?"

Melanie hesitated. "What's this about, Tess?"

Tess closed her eyes. "Please! Just tell me. Was she working the day Emily disappeared?"

She heard Melanie's quick intake of breath. "Tess? Are you asking what I think you're ask—"

"Did you see her on the playground that day? Was she anywhere near Emily?"

"God, Tess, I don't know. I don't remember. The police came to the school several times and interviewed all of us. They must know—" She broke off, drawing in another sharp breath. "She was there! I saw her when I left to go back inside. She was standing near the doorway, watching the playground—"

"I'll talk to you later," Tess said quickly.

"Tess, what are you going to do—"

She hung up the phone, gazing around the kitchen as if in some familiar corner, in some deep recess, she would find a clue to Emily's whereabouts.

She picked up the phone again to call Willa, then put it down. She picked it up again to call the police, then put it down.

What she was thinking was crazy. Willa Banks hadn't taken Emily. Why would she?

"…she's not playing with a full deck…"

"She shouldn't be allowed anywhere near those children…"

"Dear God," Tess whispered. She grabbed her keys from the counter and tore out the back door.

TESS KNEW EXACTLY where Willa lived. She'd taken her home once from the volunteer center when Willa needed a ride. It was out of Tess's way, but she'd never been that anxious to get home to an empty house, and besides, she'd felt she owed it to Willa after all she'd done to help in the search for Emily.

Now, to think that she may have been the one to take Emily—it made Tess's skin crawl. It made her sick to think that she'd been so close to Willa and hadn't suspected a thing.

Don't jump to conclusions, Tess warned herself as

she pulled to the side of road. For all she knew, Willa could be perfectly innocent, but something deep inside Tess told her that she wasn't wrong.

Set back from the main road, Willa's house was surrounded by woods, and from her upstairs windows, she'd have a view of the lake, some quarter of a mile or so to the west. Tess parked her car a hundred yards from the house, and took to the woods. She didn't want Willa to see her coming and panic.

The trees still dripped from the earlier rainstorm, and by the time Tess emerged at the back of Willa's house, her clothes were damp from the wet leaves. She stood for a moment, gazing up at the house. The lights were all out, except for a faint glow from one of the downstairs windows.

As Tess started across the yard, she fervently hoped Willa didn't have a dog. Or a gun.

A few yards from the house, she paused and glanced up. It was a dark night, but the moon was just rising over the treetops, and Tess could make out the outline of windows. One of the upstairs windows had burglar bars. Strange, because none of the downstairs windows were so equipped. Why would Willa have burglar bars at an upstairs window?

The answer almost made Tess's knees buckle. Because she wasn't trying to keep someone out. She was trying to keep someone in.

Tess's heart pounded so hard against her chest she actually felt faint. She stared up at the window, trying to peer through the darkness. And then, as if she had willed it, she saw a movement. A tiny silhouette appeared briefly at the window, and then was gone.

Emily!

JARED PULLED into Tess's driveway behind a dark blue van and got out. He started running toward the porch, but a woman's voice called to him from the van. "She's not home! I've already checked."

He retraced his footsteps to the driveway. The woman he'd seen with Tess at the volunteer center sat behind the wheel of the van. He walked slowly toward her. "You're Melanie, aren't you? Tess's friend?"

She nodded. "And you're Jared, of course. Jared Spencer." She said his name with no small amount of scorn, but then, after everything Tess had told him earlier, he could hardly blame her. "Why are you looking for Tess?"

"I need to see her. We've got some things to straighten out."

"She doesn't need to see you," Melanie said bitterly. "The best thing you can do is just leave her alone."

"I can't," Jared said. "I can't leave her alone. We have a daughter together."

Melanie gasped. Even in the darkness, Jared thought he saw her face pale. "She told you?"

"It doesn't matter how I found out. The important thing is that I know. And I'm going to do everything in my power to find Emily and bring her back home. And then I'm going to make sure my brother pays for what he did to Tess. And to you."

Melanie's eyes filled with unexpected tears. "You don't know what you're up against."

"Oh yes I do," Jared said. "Royce is the one who doesn't know."

Suddenly, all the bitterness seemed to drain out of her, and she put her head against the back of the seat, closing her eyes. "It's too late for me. Nothing will give me back my legs. Not revenge. Not justice. But you can still help Tess.'' She opened her eyes and stared at Jared. "I think she may be in real trouble."

TESS GAZED at the window, but the silhouette didn't reappear. She started to call out, but something held her back. *Don't tip off Willa. Don't do anything to endanger Emily.*

But Tess had to get her daughter out of there. She would not leave here without her, no matter what she had to do.

She tried the back entrance and found it locked.

Running around to the front, Tess flew up the porch steps and started pounding on the door. When no one answered, she banged even harder. After a few moments, the porch light came on, and Willa, dressed for bed, pulled back the door.

"Tess? What on earth—"

Tess pushed her way inside, gazing around frantically for the stairs.

Behind her Willa said anxiously, "Is something wrong?"

Tess whirled on her. "Where is she? Where's Emily? I know she's here. I saw her!"

Willa calmly closed the door and turned to Tess. "I'm afraid you're mistaken, Tess."

"I saw her! She was standing in the window upstairs!"

Willa gazed at her sadly. "You didn't see Emily, Tess. You saw Sadie."

Tess stared at her in shock. "Sadie?"

Willa's eyes brightened, and she clapped her hands together like an excited child. "Yes, isn't it wonderful? I'll be taking her home to her mother soon. Oh, I can't wait to see Naomi's face."

"Sadie," Tess said numbly. "Sadie Cross is upstairs?"

"Yes, of course. I've been waiting for just the right time to take her back home. I left that note on Naomi's Jeep so she'd know the child was close by and unharmed—"

"The note was meant for Naomi?"

"Yes! I wanted her to know that her daughter was coming home, so I had Sadie write her a message."

"You mean Emily," Tess said. "Emily wrote that note." It must have been Willa's partial fingerprint the police had found on the paper.

"No," Willa said stubbornly. "Sadie wrote that note. I watched over her while she did it."

It couldn't have been Sadie. Tess knew that. Sadie Cross had disappeared ten years ago. She would be fifteen years old now. The tiny silhouette that Tess had glimpsed in the window was much younger. A five-year-old. Emily.

Her gaze went to the stairs. "I want to see her."

"Sadie? I don't think that's a good idea. We wouldn't want to confuse her."

Tess started toward the stairs. "Emily? Emily!"

"I told you it was Sadie." The voice was right behind her, and Tess whirled, surprised that Willa was able to move so quickly. And as she turned, Willa lifted something in her hand and swung it toward Tess. She put up a hand, blocking part of the blow, but the iron poker still clipped her forehead, and Tess sank to the stairs, dazed.

Willa stood over her, her eyes—not crazed as Tess would have thought—but almost serene. Almost otherworldly. "I was at the hospital the night they took her other baby. I can't let you take Sadie."

Tess blinked, then blinked again, trying to clear her vision, her mind. Tentatively, she put a hand up to her head, and when she drew it away, her fingers were covered with blood.

"I've never forgiven myself for letting them take her baby, you see."

"Who?" Tess asked weakly.

Willa ignored her question. Her mind had gone backward in time, to another night, another tragedy. "The other woman's baby had died, and we were so afraid she wouldn't be able to handle it. And there Naomi was with two healthy baby girls. And she was so young. Just eighteen with no husband. I didn't know how she'd be able to take care of one baby, let alone two."

"What happened?" Tess asked softly.

"'No one will ever know,'" she said in a different voice. "But I knew. I couldn't forget. I used to dream about that baby every night. Sometimes I even thought I could hear her cry. And then when Sadie disappeared, I couldn't believe the fates could be so cruel. Why did Naomi have to lose both her children?"

Tess eased herself up on her elbows. "Did you take Sadie?"

Willa blinked in confusion. "Take Sadie? Why on earth would you think such a thing? No, of course I didn't take Sadie. I ached for her poor mother. I prayed that she would be returned to her, and then she was. When I saw her on the playground that day, with her little brown eyes and dark hair, it was like a miracle had happened. Sadie had come back, and I could take her home to her mother. I could finally make things right with Naomi."

She's deranged, delusional, and God knows what

else, Tess thought. But she couldn't worry about Willa's mental state. She couldn't worry about her motive in taking Emily. Emily was somewhere in this house. That was all that mattered. All that Tess could afford to focus on.

Her mind and vision clearing, she eased herself up. Willa held the iron poker down by her side, still at the ready, but this time she no longer had the element of surprise. Tess waited for a moment, gathering her strength, and then she lunged at the older woman, toppling them both backward down the stairs. They crashed into the wall, and Willa slumped to the floor.

Tess left her where she fell. She turned and ran up the steps, calling frantically to Emily. She tried every door upstairs until she found one that was locked. "Emily?"

Very faintly a sound came to her. Tess pressed her ear against the door.

"Mama! Mama!"

Tess's heart almost fought its way out of her chest. She frantically shook the knob, then pushed against the door. When it wouldn't open, she glanced around for a battering ram. "Emily! Mama's here, baby. I'm going to get you out."

More clearly now, as if her daughter were pressed against the door. "Mama!"

For a moment, Tess pressed her cheek against the wood, knowing that her daughter was on the other side. She wanted to claw the door open with her bare hands, but instead she ran downstairs and grabbed the poker from Willa's hand. The woman groaned, but Tess gave her barely a glance. She flew back upstairs and said through the wood, "Step away from the door, Emily. Okay?"

"Yes, Mama." Then, more faintly. "Okay."

Like a crazy woman, Tess beat at the lock, then used the poker as a wedge between the door and the jamb. Within moments, she was gasping from her frenzied efforts, almost sobbing in frustration, but the door finally sprang free. She threw down the poker and stepped inside.

The room was dark, but Emily stood at the window, back lit by the moon.

"Emily?"

"Mama? Mama!"

Tess rushed toward her as Emily launched herself forward. They met in the middle of the room, and Tess fell to her knees, grabbing blindly for her daughter.

"Emily, Emily!" She scooped Emily into her arms, holding her tight, her eyes burning with tears. "Mama's here, baby! I'm finally here!"

Chapter Fourteen

"Mama?"

Emily drew back slightly, patting Tess's hair, cupping her face in her little hands. *"Mama,"* she said in wonder, as if she couldn't believe her own eyes.

"Yes, baby, it's me." Tess forced back her tears as she planted tiny kisses on Emily's nose, her chin, and in her hair. "I'm going to take you home."

"Home." Emily started to cry then, and she wrapped her arms tightly around Tess's neck, laying her head on her shoulder. Her little chest heaved up and down with her sobs. "I—I didn't think you were c-coming."

"I know, honey, shush." Tess smoothed her hand down Emily's hair.

"Sh-she kept showing me a pi-picture of this lady. She s-said it was my m-mama. But it w-wasn't you. I was s-so afraid—"

"I know, baby. I know."

"I was a-afraid you were in h-heaven with G-Grandpa, and I was g-going to have a n-new mama."

"Oh, Emily, no. No, sweetie, I'm fine." Tess pried Emily's arms from her neck and held her sweet little face, wiping away her daughter's tears. "I'm here now, and I'm going to take you home."

"F-forever?"

"Yes, baby. Forever."

Emily lay her head on Tess's shoulder again, but suddenly she stiffened. She stepped back, her eyes filled with confusion. "Who's that woman?"

Tess turned. In her joy, she'd momentarily forgotten about Willa Banks.

But it wasn't the older woman who stood in the doorway. It was Ariel Spencer, and she had a gun pointed directly at Tess and Emily.

Her heart pounding in terror, Tess rose and put Emily behind her.

Ariel was a small woman, but the gun gave her formidable power and she seemed to know this. She gestured with the barrel toward Emily. "I'm sorry, but I can't let her be found."

Tess stared at her across the room, gauging the distance, analyzing the risk of getting to Ariel before she could fire the weapon. Her chances weren't good, she knew. And if Tess went down, nothing stood between the gun and Emily.

"Why?" she asked helplessly.

"Because I don't want to lose my husband," Ariel said angrily. "If he loses the trust, what reason would he have for staying with me and the children?"

The trust again. The money that had already led to violence. This was Davis Spencer's legacy. To make his sons so competitive they would do anything to win. But Jared wasn't like that. And it wasn't Royce who stood before Tess now.

Ariel shook her head sadly. "He didn't love me when we married. It was all about the money. I knew that. But I thought in time—'' She broke off, taking a step into the room. In the moonlight, her face looked thin and ghostly. ''He couldn't love me, you see, because he was in love with you.''

Tess gasped. ''No! That's not true. He hardly knew me.''

''I saw the way he looked at you. The way his eyes followed you around that night. I saw in his eyes what I never saw when he looked at me.'' She paused, her gaze narrowing in the darkness. ''I saw Royce and that…slut down by the lake that night. I knew they were planning to meet later, and I knew I would have to put a stop to it. But even so, she wasn't the one I was worried about. I knew she was just another of his conquests. You were the one I had to get rid of.

''When I came back down to the lake to confront her and Royce, I saw you talking to her. When you got in her car, I followed you. I thought, 'Here's my chance to get rid of both of them.' It seemed so easy, so perfect. My only mistake was that I didn't stay and make certain everything…was taken care of. But I had to get back to the house before I was missed. I had to be there when Royce set his plan in motion.''

''The bracelet, you mean,'' Tess said. Her mind reeled with everything Ariel had told her, but she tried to brush it aside. She had to keep a clear head. She had to find a way out of this. She had to protect Emily at any cost.

''Come on,'' Ariel said. ''We're all going to take a little drive.'' When Tess hesitated, Ariel lifted the gun. ''I don't want to do it this way, but I will if I have to.''

Tess took Emily's hand. ''Come on, sweetie,'' she murmured.

Emily hung back. "I'm scared."

"It'll be okay. I promise." Tess prayed it was a promise she would be able to keep.

Ariel motioned for them to go first, and Tess, clinging to Emily's hand, walked slowly out the door and then down the stairs, all the while gazing around for a weapon, a diversion, anything that would allow her to get Emily away.

Willa still lay unconscious at the bottom of the stairs. When Emily saw her, she faltered and hung back, and Tess knelt to reassure her. She hugged her close, whispering in her ear, "When I say run, go out the front door, Emily. Run as fast as you can. Find a place in the woods to hide. Whatever you do, don't look back. Understand?"

Emily nodded.

"What are you telling her?" Ariel demanded.

Tess glanced up. "I was telling her that everything would be okay. The same thing you would be telling your children if you were in my place," she said angrily, hoping to appeal to Ariel's maternal instincts, if nothing else.

For a moment, Tess thought it might work. A look of despair came over Ariel's plain features, then her gaze hardened. "I'm doing this for my children. My son is the first Spencer grandchild. He's entitled to that trust, and I won't let anyone take it away from him. I won't let anyone destroy my family."

"But you're willing to destroy mine," Tess said on a whisper. Slowly she stood to face Ariel. Putting herself once again between Emily and the gun, Tess grew suddenly calm, knowing exactly what she had to do. Images of her daughter flashed like a strobe through her mind. Emily, on the day she was born, clutching

Tess's finger. Emily, taking her first step. Emily, saying mama for the first time. Emily, starting kindergarten. Emily, one of the special ones. Emily, with her whole future ahead of her.

Her mind flashed forward, and she saw Emily graduating from high school. From college. Emily, in a wedding dress…all the things that Tess would never see. A terrible sadness came over her, but she gathered her strength and courage.

"Now, Emily, now!" she screamed as she lunged toward the stairs. "Run!"

Ariel, stunned by the sudden attack, stumbled backward, grabbing hold of the stair railing to steady herself. But she never lost control of her weapon. Before Tess could reach her, she lifted the gun and fired.

PEERING FROM BEHIND the dripping branches of a bush, Emily clutched Brown Bear tightly in her arms as she watched the woman with the gun come running into the woods. Emily hadn't gotten very far into the trees when she'd heard the sound of footsteps behind her. She'd plunged into a thicket of bushes and tried to remain as still as she could, but she couldn't control her trembling.

"Emily!" the woman called. "Where are you, baby? It's Mama."

Emily's heart began to pound wildly. For a moment, she almost let herself hope that it was her mama who was calling to her. She even half stood from her hiding spot, but then she sank back down. She hadn't let herself be fooled by that woman in the picture, and she wouldn't be fooled now.

She would wait. Mama would come for her again. She had to.

But…where was Mama? And what was that loud noise Emily had heard as she'd torn across the yard toward the woods?

She hadn't looked back to find out. She hadn't dared look back. Mama had told her to run as fast as she could, and that's what Emily had done. But what was she supposed to do now?

What if she had to stay out here all night? Emily couldn't bear that thought. Her arms and legs stung from a million mosquito bites, and she could hear the pesky insects even now swarming around her head. But she didn't dare swat them away.

"Emily!"

She eased forward, just a tiny bit, until she could see between the branches. She almost gasped in shock, and her hand went automatically to her mouth to keep from making a noise. The woman with the gun stood right in front of the thicket where Emily was hidden. She was so close Emily could reach out and touch her.

The woman moved a few steps away. "Emily! Come out now. You can't stay out here all night!"

She didn't want to stay out here all night. The mosquitoes were bad enough, but what if there were snakes, not the kind that had gotten into their house once, but the other kind? The kind that bit you and made you sick, and then you died. Copperheads and water moccasins. Emily knew about those snakes because Mama had told her about them when they'd gone walking together in the woods behind their house. She'd taught her about poison ivy, too. There was even a little poem. *Leaves of three, let it be.*

Maybe that was why her legs itched so badly, Emily thought. Maybe she was sitting right in the middle of a poison-ivy patch. The more she thought about it, the more her legs itched.

"Emily! I have a little boy your age. He always does what I tell him. He knows better than to disobey me. Come out, now. Do as I say, and I'll take you to your mama."

Emily squeezed her eyes shut, as if she could blot out the woman's voice. The almost irresistible temptation she offered.

"Your mama's going to be real mad at you if you don't come out."

The mosquito bites were becoming unbearable now. Emily eased her hand down to the side of her leg, but as she shifted her position, her knee pressed down on a dead twig, snapping it in two. Emily froze.

Through the leaves, she saw the woman whirl and start toward her. The gun in her hand gleamed menacingly in the moonlight. Emily had never seen a real gun this close before, but she knew about them. She knew what they could do. She hunkered down in the shadows of the bushes, her heartbeat pounding in her ears.

After a moment, she glanced up. The woman had moved away from her and was using the gun to poke at some bushes. Then she disappeared from Emily's line of sight.

Emily looked back at the house, her prison just a little while ago, but now she was drawn inexorably to the light pooling from the windows. Mama might still be in there. She might even now be waiting for Emily to come back.

"Emily!"

A warm, stray breeze carried her name back to her. The sound was distant, fleeting. She glanced back at the house. Scrambling out of her hiding place, she stood. And only then did she realize that someone else was in the woods. Only then did she realize that a new danger stood between her and the house.

TESS LAY at the foot of the stairs, reclining against the bottom step as she surveyed the hole in her shoulder. Too high to have hit her heart, she decided. Too far over to have nicked a lung. Still, it was more than a flesh wound. Tess knew she was badly hurt, and judging by the size of the crimson bloom on her clothing and on the floor, if the wound didn't kill her the loss of blood just might.

She struggled to sit up. Willa was nowhere in sight, and for a moment Tess nursed the hope that she'd gone to protect Emily. But Willa was the one who had kidnapped Emily from school. Willa was the one who had held her prisoner here for a month. Melanie had told Tess that the police had interviewed the Fairhaven staff and faculty several times at school, but if only they'd come here to talk to Willa! They might have found Emily sooner. She might now be safe instead of pursued by a mad woman.

But it was Ariel Spencer who wanted Emily dead.

Using the banister, Tess pulled herself up, clinging for a moment as a spell of dizziness threatened to fell her again. Gritting her teeth, she staggered to the door, opened it and stumbled outside. She fell on the porch steps and tumbled the rest of the way to the ground, rolling on her back as she gazed up at the stars that had twinkled out since the storm.

Her mind grew foggy, and suddenly she had no deeper ambition than to lie on the wet ground forever, watching those stars. She and Jared had made Emily under those same stars—

Jared.

Emily.

Her daughter was out there somewhere, with no one to save her but Tess.

Struggling to her feet, she tried to remember where she'd told Emily to run.

JARED STARED DOWN into Emily's little face, his heart hammering like a piston inside him. He'd never seen his daughter before, but he would have known her anywhere. The urge to scoop her up and hold her tight was almost overwhelming, but the fear in her eyes stopped him.

He'd seen Tess's truck parked down the road, and he'd pulled his car in behind it. As he'd walked toward the house, he'd seen a tiny figure, hardly more than a blur, launch herself across the yard and disappear into the woods. And as he'd started toward her, he'd seen another figure, a woman running after her. He'd thought at first it was Tess, and had wanted to call out, but then, as moonlight had slanted over the woman's features, he'd recognized Ariel.

He hadn't stopped to wonder why his brother's wife was at Willa Banks's house. Some long-buried instinct had told him what he needed to know. His daughter was in danger, and Jared had plunged into the woods after them.

He knelt and put his finger to his lips. "It's okay," he whispered. "I'm not going to hurt you." He could see that she was trembling, but he didn't dare touch her. She might scream, and Jared had seen something else in the moonlight before Ariel had entered the woods. She had a gun.

It had something to do with the trust. Jared knew that, but he didn't have time to worry about the details. He had to get Emily to safety. And then he had to find Tess. If he wasn't too late.

Emily was steadily inching away from him, and he knew at any moment she might bolt. Or call out. He had to do something quickly to win her trust, and there was only one thing Jared could think of that might work.

"Emily," he whispered. "I'm your father. I won't hurt you, I promise."

Her dark little eyes widened. "You're...my daddy?"

He nodded.

"Did you come to rescue me?" she asked in a whispery little voice.

Jared's throat tightened. "Yes." He reached out a hand and, after a moment's hesitation, she slipped her tiny one into his. And at that exact moment, Ariel came scrambling up an embankment behind them.

Emily screamed, and Jared automatically pushed her behind him. Ariel's clothing was filthy and torn, and her face and arms were scratched and bleeding. Panting hard, she looked like a wild woman, but her eyes were what sent a cold chill racing up Jared's spine. Her eyes, even in the darkness, seemed to glow with a madness that was completely out of control.

"Ariel," he said softly. "You don't have to do this."

"You always bested him in everything," she said contemptuously. "You always had to make him look bad in your father's eyes. I won't let you take that trust away from him, Jared. I won't.''

''I don't want the trust,'' Jared said, trying to keep his voice calm. He reached behind him, and almost instantly, he felt Emily's hand slip into his. He closed his fingers around hers, trying to reassure her.

''It doesn't matter whether you want it or not. Your father's terms are clear. The trust goes to the first Spencer grandchild. Her.'' She motioned with the gun behind Jared. ''I knew the moment I saw her picture in your office that day that it would come to this.''

''It doesn't have to be this way, Ariel. Think about your own children, what this will do to them.''

''How dare you?'' she said through clenched teeth. ''I *am* thinking about my children. They're why I'm doing this. I don't want them to lose their father.''

''You think Royce would leave you if he lost the trust?'' Jared said incredulously. ''He wouldn't. He loves you.''

''No,'' Ariel said angrily. ''He doesn't. He never has. He loves her.'' She nodded over her shoulder toward the house. ''But I've taken care of that, too. This time, she won't be coming back. Ever.''

Jared's heart dropped like a stone inside his chest. What did she mean, Tess wouldn't be coming back? No, he thought. Please, no.

He couldn't allow himself to think about Tess now. He had to think of Emily. He had to get her out of this.

''Ariel, please. Just put down the gun. You don't want to do this.''

''I may not want to, but it has to be done. I've come too far now.''

''Ariel—''

Something snapped in the woods to her right, and

Ariel spun, firing wildly at the sound. Jared sprang toward her, and as she whipped the gun back around, he grabbed her wrist, jerking it skyward so that the second shot missed Emily by a mile. He heard her scream anyway, and the sound tore something lose inside him. Almost viciously, he wrested the gun from Ariel's hand and flung her aside. She stumbled backward, losing her footing on the wet ground.

Her body hit the ground with a jarring thud, and then she rolled down the embankment with surprising speed. Another thud, and then all was silent.

Jared turned to Emily. "Wait here," he said grimly. "Okay?"

He scrambled down the embankment after Ariel, wanting to make certain that she would not pose a further threat. But he needn't have worried. A boulder had stopped her progression down the hill, and he could tell from the odd angle of her head that her neck was broken.

He struggled back up the incline to Emily. When he got to the top, she was kneeling on the ground, cradling Tess's head in her lap. "Mama's hurt," she said, and then began to cry.

Chapter Fifteen

It was three days later before Tess was wholly conscious of everything going on around her. She'd undergone surgery within an hour of arriving at the hospital, and then had spent the next twenty-four hours in recovery and intensive care before being moved to a private room on the fourth floor.

During that time, she'd been aware only vaguely of people coming into her room. Doctors and nurses. Her mother. Melanie. Jared? Or had his presence been her imagination? She thought she'd seen him sitting by her bed once, talking to her in a low voice about the past and the future. Imploring her to wake up. Promising her that she and Emily were the only family that mattered to him.

And the police had come, of course, but Tess couldn't remember what she'd told them. She couldn't remember much of anything. She'd been too hazy from the drugs and too exhausted from the surgery to distinguish between reality and her dreamworld.

Today, however, she'd actually gotten out of bed with the help of two nurses and taken a walk down the hallway. The nurses had applauded her efforts even though her legs had shaken like Jell-O every step of the way, and they'd had to help her back to bed.

She relaxed against her pillows now and tried to ignore the nagging pain in her shoulder as she glanced up at Abby and Naomi Cross.

"So," Abby was saying, "that's where we stand right now. We're running a full background check on Willa Banks, and, of course, we'll search the hospital files from the night that Naomi gave birth. But as you might expect, the records are pretty chaotic. Over a hundred people were brought in to the hospital that night, and one of the fatalities was a doctor on staff. Two more were seriously injured. They were so shorthanded that night that it's easy to see how someone intent on stealing a baby could have gotten away with it."

Tess's gaze met Naomi's. "I'm so sorry I can't tell you anything more." And neither, unfortunately, could Willa Banks. She'd suffered a massive heart attack that night, and her body had been found in the woods by the police. Tess was convinced she'd been trying to get to Emily, maybe to save her, but pity, let alone gratitude, was still something Tess had a hard time mustering for Willa Banks.

Naomi placed her hand over Tess's. "Don't be sorry. If it wasn't for you, I'd never have known about my baby. I'd never have known that one of my little girls is still out there somewhere."

"One?" Tess asked, glancing at Abby.

Abby's expression grew shuttered. "We still don't know about the remains that were found in Grover County. The identification process could take a while."

"I'm sorry," she said again to Naomi.

Naomi's smile was the saddest thing Tess had ever

seen. "If it is Sadie, then at least I'll finally be able to bring her back home."

Tess's eyes filled with tears. She wished with all her heart that Naomi's story could have turned out the way hers had. She wished every missing child could have a happy ending, but in the real world, it didn't always work out that way. She was lucky. Very, very lucky, and she would never stop giving thanks until the day she died.

"In the meantime," Naomi said, "I'm going to search for my other baby. And I won't give up until I find her."

Worry flickered across Abby's forehead as she took Naomi's arm. "Let's just take it one step at a time, okay? Right now, we'd better let Tess get some rest."

Naomi gave Tess a wry smile. "Her beau's in town. That's why she's so anxious to leave."

A becoming blush tinged Abby's cheeks. "Honestly, Naomi, my *beau?* You sound like you were born two centuries ago."

"Spoken like a true modern woman living in sin."

The blush on Abby's cheeks deepened. "I am not living in sin. Sam and I are taking things nice and slow."

"Sam?" Tess asked.

"Sam Burke. The profiler," Naomi said, grinning. "He got Abby into the FBI Academy. She's going to be leaving in two weeks."

"He did no such thing! I got in on my own merits," Abby insisted, but Tess could tell the argument on both sides was good-natured. She could see the glow of pride in Naomi's eyes when she looked at her sister. And the glow of newfound love in Abby's eyes when she spoke of Sam Burke. Tess envied her. She wished that she and Jared were embarking on a new relationship, a new beginning, but after all the secrets, after all the lies, Tess was very much afraid a future for them still wasn't in the cards.

After Abby and Naomi left, Tess dozed for a while, awakening in the middle of the afternoon to a strange, tingling sensation along her arm. And the wonderful sound of little-girl laughter. She opened her eyes and saw Emily perched on the edge of the bed, both hands clapped to her mouth as she tried to suppress her giggles. Beside Tess's arm lay a feather. And behind Emily stood Jared.

Tess blinked, trying to bring them both into focus more clearly. Emily had been staying with Tess's mother while Tess was in the hospital. So what was she doing here with Jared? Not that Tess would ever try to keep them apart now that the danger had passed. Ariel was dead, and during one of Tess's more lucid moments after surgery, her mother had told her that she'd heard Royce was taking his children away for a long vacation after the funeral in order to protect them from all the publicity.

Hard to think of Royce in the role of protector, Tess thought. Hard to imagine Jared here with Emily. It was all just so...strange.

"You awake, Mama?"

"I am now," she murmured. She opened her arms and Emily snuggled down against her, hugging her tight. It felt so wonderful to hold her daughter again. Emily didn't understand why she'd been kidnapped by Willa Banks. Why Ariel Spencer, a woman she'd never seen before, had wanted to hurt her. She had no idea that someday, as the first Spencer grandchild, she would be a very rich young woman. For now she was content to snuggle in her mother's arms, safe, protected, loved.

And Tess never wanted to let her go.

Emily wiggled a bit and Tess winced from the contact. Jared said, "Careful now."

Emily started to pull away, but Tess held on to her. "That's okay, sweetie," she said, burying her face in Emily's hair, reveling in the sweet feel of her daughter in her arms. "You just keep right on hugging me. As tight as you want."

But Emily broke loose and sat back up. "This is Jared, Mama."

Tess looked at Jared, then glanced away. So much had happened. So many emotions. She cleared her throat. "Yes, I know."

"Did you know he's my daddy?" Emily asked innocently.

Tess felt her heart leaped wildly inside her chest. "Wh-what makes you think that?"

"He told me."

Tess's gaze flew to Jared. He had no right. It should have been her decision. They should have told her together.

"I had to," he said softly. "I wanted her to trust me."

"Yes," Emily agreed. "He had to so I wouldn't scream, and so the lady wouldn't shoot me."

Her casual words made Tess want to cry. She blinked back her tears, but Emily noticed and she leaned down to hug Tess again.

"Mama, don't cry. Having a daddy is a good thing. I prayed and prayed for one to come and rescue me when I was locked in that room, and he did." She turned and beamed at Jared.

He had to blink back his own tears, Tess noticed.

Emily put her lips against Tess's ear and whispered, "He's strong, Mama. Very, very strong. If you let him come and live with us, we wouldn't ever have to be afraid again."

Tess couldn't keep the tears from flowing then. She hugged Emily to her, wishing that life could be as simple as her daughter made it sound. But Jared might not want to come and live with them. He might want to be Emily's daddy without being Tess's husband. After everything that had happened between them, he still might not think her worth the trouble.

And there would be trouble. They came from two different worlds, she and Jared. They were never meant to be together. Maybe Jared realized that now.

She looked up, finally, and met his gaze. The answer to all her questions, to all her prayers, was there in his deep, dark eyes.

He took her hand and lifted it to his lips. "You and Emily are my family, Tess. Do you understand what I mean?"

She nodded, her throat tight.

"Good," he said. "Because now that I've found you, I don't ever intend to let you go."

He bent and kissed her, and Emily's giggle was the sweetest sound Tess had ever heard.

Don't miss the final installment of
EDEN'S CHILDREN,
a gripping trilogy
by Amanda Stevens.

Look for
THE FORGIVEN
next month wherever
Harlequin books are sold.

Prologue

Eden, Mississippi

*"...National Weather Service has issued a tornado
warning for the northeastern portion of Jefferson
County. A funnel cloud was reported on the ground
near Eden at approximately 8:37 this evening. If you
are in the designated area, you are urged to take cover
immediately. Repeat. A tornado warning has been issued—"*

Eighteen-year-old Naomi Cross strained to hear the
weather advisory over the static on her car radio. A
shudder of fear ripped through her as a siren blasted a
warning in the distance. But she kept on driving. Storm
or no storm, she had to get to the hospital.

As she cast an uneasy glance toward the sky, she
felt a tightening in her abdomen and braced herself,
trying to will away the intense pain she knew would
follow. She was still a good twenty minutes from the
hospital, and the contractions were hitting her hard and
fast. Too fast. The twins were coming early. The doctor
had said that might happen. But tonight of all nights!

Her mother and sister had driven down to Jackson
for a basketball tournament, and wouldn't be back until

after midnight. Naomi had been home alone as she'd listened to the increasingly severe weather reports on the news. Then the wind had started to blow, and the power went out. By the time the first contraction hit, the phone lines were down. Naomi, trying desperately not to panic, had surveyed her options—try to wait out the storm, or drive herself to the hospital.

Not much of a choice, considering Dr. Simms had warned her that multiple births were often a tricky business. Naomi didn't dare risk her babies' health by going through labor all alone, but now, as she plunged headlong into the storm, she had to wonder if she'd made the right decision. She could feel the gusts of wind tugging at her car, and it was all she could do to keep the vehicle on the road.

Gripping the steering wheel, she peered straight ahead. A wicker rocking chair, swept from someone's front porch, tumbled along the shoulder of the road, and moments later, parts of the front porch landed with a thud on the highway directly in front of her, blocking her path.

She swerved and braked, then sat for a moment, heart pounding like a kettledrum. Shoving the gearshift into park, she got out of the car. The wind tore at her hair and clothing, almost knocking her off her feet. Battling against the gale force, she fought her way to the front of the car, then lifted the two-by-fours and dragged them from the road. As she turned back to the car, a contraction bent her double.

Leaning heavily against the front fender of the car, Naomi struggled to control the pain. Somewhere off to her right, she heard the loud *crack* of an uprooting tree, and as she turned toward the sound, her breath caught in her throat.

For what seemed like an eternity, she stared, paralyzed, at the funnel cloud moving toward her. She'd never seen anything like it! The size. The sheer force. The deafening roar as the twister whirled across a field, claiming everything in its path.

The roof of an old barn peeled away as cleanly as the lid on a tin can, and the walls crumpled. Fence posts were sucked from the ground and tossed fifty yards away. And still the storm came.

Get back in the car! a voice screamed inside Naomi. *Move!*

The wind almost whipped the car door from its hinges as she climbed back inside. Using both hands, she finally managed to slam the door, and then, with one last glance at the tornado, moving with frightening speed across the open ground, she put the car in gear and pressed the accelerator. The car shot forward, almost slamming into a sheet of tin roofing that spun like a giant Frisbee in the wind. At the last moment, the metal lifted, just missing the top of the car and swirled away.

On the radio, the announcer's excited voice, intermixed with the static, drew icy fingers of dread down Naomi's back.

"If you are...path of...storm...seek shelter immediately! Repeat. ...shelter immediately—"

Naomi glanced around frantically. She was in the middle of nowhere. Still miles from town. No houses in sight. No overpasses. On the flat highway, she was helpless.

She glanced at the field to her right. *Oh, God. Oh, dear God.*

The storm was so close...she could feel the pressure building inside the car...could feel the automobile being pulled off the road...

Her hands clutched the steering wheel. Faster, she urged. Faster.

Please. Oh, please.

Never, ever try to outrun a tornado, she'd always been told. Now she knew why. Her puny car was no match for such power. She was going to be swept off the road, swirled up into the vortex of the storm.

My babies…

Faster. *Come on.* Faster. *Please. Please…*

Her knuckles ached from gripping the wheel. She felt the familiar tightening in her stomach that signaled another contraction. *No. Oh, no…*

She gasped out loud from the pain, but somehow she managed to hold on. Somehow she managed to keep control of the car.

She glanced out the window. The twister was right there. Right on her. *Oh, God, oh, God, oh, God!*

Something hit the back window, and the glass shattered into a million pieces. The din from the storm was thunderous. The suction incredible. Naomi grasped the wheel for dear life as she floored the accelerator. The car swayed in the wind. Debris whirled thick outside her windows.

Glancing in the rearview mirror, she saw the funnel pass across the highway behind her. But for a moment, as the sound dissipated and the pressure inside the car decreased, Naomi still couldn't breathe. She still couldn't comprehend that she had outrun a tornado, that she might yet make it to the hospital to have her babies. Then, sobbing in relief, she said a silent prayer as she raced toward Eden.

By the time she reached town, the streets resembled a war zone, but she didn't stop to assess the damage. The contractions were getting closer with each passing moment, and she knew she wouldn't be able to hang on much longer.

As she pulled into the emergency area of the tiny hospital, she all but tumbled from the car. Clutching her stomach, she lurched inside, seeking help, but the emergency room was in chaos. Bodies lay everywhere, some moving, some not. And the wails—of terror, of grief, of disbelief—were the sounds of a nightmare come to life.

"Please," Naomi said to one of the harried nurses. "Help me."

The woman turned, as if to brush Naomi aside, but then her gaze dropped and her eyes widened. "Get a gurney over here, stat!" she shouted.

It was only then that Naomi looked down to see blood pooling at her feet.

She was dimly aware of being lifted, of being rushed down a long corridor with the echo of madness in her ears.

One of the nurses said in a hushed tone, "We've got another mother prepped for O.R., but we still haven't heard from Dr. Simms."

"How's she doing?" someone else asked worriedly.

"Not good. We're having trouble finding the baby's heartbeat—"

Naomi tried to lift her head. "My babies—"

"Shush," the first nurse soothed. "Not you. You're doing fine. Just try to relax."

And then another voice, from a distance, shouted, "Oh my God, there's a second one!"

Yes, Naomi thought in a haze of pain. *I'm having twins.*

"Another tornado!" the voice screamed.

And then the walls began to tremble…

AND YOU THOUGHT TEXAS WAS BIG!

HARLEQUIN®
INTRIGUE®

continues its most secret, seriously sinister and deadly *confidential* series in the Big Sky state with four more sexy cowboy agents guaranteed to take your breath away!

Men bound by love, loyalty and the law—these specialized government operatives have vowed to keep their missions and identities confidential....

SOMEONE TO PROTECT HER
PATRICIA ROSEMOOR
September 2001

SPECIAL ASSIGNMENT: BABY
DEBRA WEBB
October 2001

LICENSED TO MARRY
CHARLOTTE DOUGLAS
November 2001

SECRET AGENT HEIRESS
JULIE MILLER
December 2001

Available wherever Harlequin books are sold.

HARLEQUIN®
Makes any time special ®

*Harlequin truly does
make any time special....
This year we are celebrating
weddings in style!*

To help us celebrate, we want you to tell us how wearing the Harlequin wedding gown will make your wedding day special. As the grand prize, Harlequin will offer one lucky bride the chance to **"Walk Down the Aisle"** in the Harlequin wedding gown!

There's more...

For her honeymoon, she and her groom will spend five nights at the **Hyatt Regency Maui.** As part of this five-night honeymoon at the hotel renowned for its romantic attractions, the couple will enjoy a candlelit dinner for two in Swan Court, a sunset sail on the hotel's catamaran, and duet spa treatments.

To enter, please write, in, 250 words or less, how wearing the Harlequin wedding gown will make your wedding day special. The entry will be judged based on its emotionally compelling nature, its originality and creativity, and its sincerity. This contest is open to Canadian and U.S. residents only and to those who are 18 years of age and older. There is no purchase necessary to enter. Void where prohibited. See further contest rules attached. Please send your entry to:

Walk Down the Aisle Contest

In Canada	In U.S.A.
P.O. Box 637	P.O. Box 9076
Fort Erie, Ontario	3010 Walden Ave.
L2A 5X3	Buffalo, NY 14269-9076

You can also enter by visiting www.eHarlequin.com
Win the Harlequin wedding gown and the vacation of a lifetime!
The deadline for entries is October 1, 2001.

PHWDACONT1

1. To enter, follow directions published in the offer to which you are responding. Contest begins April 2, 2001, and ends on October 1, 2001. Method of entry may vary. Mailed entries must be postmarked by October 1, 2001, and received by October 8, 2001.

2. Contest entry may be, at times, presented via the Internet, but will be restricted solely to residents of certain georgraphic areas that are disclosed on the Web site. To enter via the Internet, if permissible, access the Harlequin Web site (www.eHarlequin.com) and follow the directions displayed online. Online entries must be received by 11:59 p.m. E.S.T. on October 1, 2001.

   In lieu of submitting an entry online, enter by mail by hand-printing (or typing) on an 8¹/₂" x 11" plain piece of paper, your name, address (including zip code), Contest number/name and in 250 words or fewer, why winning a Harlequin wedding dress would make your wedding day special. Mail via first-class mail to: Harlequin Walk Down the Aisle Contest 1197, (in the U.S.) P.O. Box 9076, 3010 Walden Avenue, Buffalo, NY 14269-9076, (in Canada) P.O. Box 637, Fort Erie, Ontario L2A 5X3, Canada.

   Limit one entry per person, household address and e-mail address. Online and/or mailed entries received from persons residing in geographic areas in which Internet entry is not permissible will be disqualified.

3. Contests will be judged by a panel of members of the Harlequin editorial, marketing and public relations staff based on the following criteria:

   - Originality and Creativity—50%
   - Emotionally Compelling—25%
   - Sincerity—25%

   In the event of a tie, duplicate prizes will be awarded. Decisions of the judges are final.

4. All entries become the property of Torstar Corp. and will not be returned. No responsibility is assumed for lost, late, illegible, incomplete, inaccurate, nondelivered or misdirected mail or misdirected e-mail, for technical, hardware or software failures of any kind, lost or unavailable network connections, or failed, incomplete, garbled or delayed computer transmission or any human error which may occur in the receipt or processing of the entries in this Contest.

5. Contest open only to residents of the U.S. (except Puerto Rico) and Canada, who are 18 years of age or older, and is void wherever prohibited by law; all applicable laws and regulations apply. Any litigation within the Province of Quebec respecting the conduct or organization of a publicity contest may be submitted to the Régie des alcools, des courses et des jeux for a ruling. Any litigation respecting the awarding of a prize may be submitted to the Régie des alcools, des courses et des jeux only for the purpose of helping the parties reach a settlement. Employees and immediate family members of Torstar Corp. and D. L. Blair, Inc., their affiliates, subsidiaries and all other agencies, entities and persons connected with the use, marketing or conduct of this Contest are not eligible to enter. Taxes on prizes are the sole responsibility of winners. Acceptance of any prize offered constitutes permission to use winner's name, photograph or other likeness for the purposes of advertising, trade and promotion on behalf of Torstar Corp., its affiliates and subsidiaries without further compensation to the winner, unless prohibited by law.

6. Winners will be determined no later than November 15, 2001, and will be notified by mail. Winners will be required to sign and return an Affidavit of Eligibility form within 15 days after winner notification. Noncompliance within that time period may result in disqualification and an alternative winner may be selected. Winners of trip must execute a Release of Liability prior to ticketing and must possess required travel documents (e.g. passport, photo ID) where applicable. Trip must be completed by November 2002. No substitution of prize permitted by winner. Torstar Corp. and D. L. Blair, Inc., their parents, affiliates, and subsidiaries are not responsible for errors in printing or electronic presentation of Contest, entries and/or game pieces. In the event of printing or other errors which may result in unintended prize values or duplication of prizes, all affected game pieces or entries shall be null and void. If for any reason the Internet portion of the Contest is not capable of running as planned, including infection by computer virus, bugs, tampering, unauthorized intervention, fraud, technical failures, or any other causes beyond the control of Torstar Corp. which corrupt or affect the administration, secrecy, fairness, integrity or proper conduct of the Contest, Torstar Corp. reserves the right, at its sole discretion, to disqualify any individual who tampers with the entry process and to cancel, terminate, modify or suspend the Contest or the Internet portion thereof. In the event of a dispute regarding an online entry, the entry will be deemed submitted by the authorized holder of the e-mail account submitted at the time of entry. Authorized account holder is defined as the natural person who is assigned to an e-mail address by an Internet access provider, online service provider or other organization that is responsible for arranging e-mail address for the domain associated with the submitted e-mail address. **Purchase or acceptance of a product offer does not improve your chances of winning.**

7. Prizes: (1) Grand Prize—A Harlequin wedding dress (approximate retail value: $3,500) and a 5-night/6-day honeymoon trip to Maui, HI, including round-trip air transportation provided by Maui Visitors Bureau from Los Angeles International Airport (winner is responsible for transportation to and from Los Angeles International Airport) and a Harlequin Romance Package, including hotel accomodations (double occupancy) at the Hyatt Regency Maui Resort and Spa, dinner for (2) two at Swan Court, a sunset sail on Kiele V and a spa treatment for the winner (approximate retail value: $4,000); (5) Five runner-up prizes of a $1000 gift certificate to selected retail outlets to be determined by Sponsor (retail value $1000 ea.). Prizes consist of only those items listed as part of the prize. Limit one prize per person. All prizes are valued in U.S. currency.

8. For a list of winners (available after December 17, 2001) send a self-addressed, stamped envelope to: Harlequin Walk Down the Aisle Contest 1197 Winners, P.O. Box 4200 Blair, NE 68009-4200 or you may access the www.eHarlequin.com Web site through January 15, 2002.

Contest sponsored by Torstar Corp., P.O. Box 9042, Buffalo, NY 14269-9042, U.S.A.

PHWDACONT2

COMING SOON...

AN EXCITING
OPPORTUNITY TO SAVE
ON THE PURCHASE OF
HARLEQUIN AND
SILHOUETTE BOOKS!

*DETAILS TO FOLLOW
IN OCTOBER 2001!*

YOU WON'T WANT TO MISS IT!

PHQ401